KING OF THE MOLE PEOPLE

KING OF THE MOLE PEOPLE

BOOK 1

PAUL GILLIGAN

Christy Ottaviano Books

HENRY HOLT AND COMPANY

NEW YORK

Henry Holt and Company, *Publishers since 1866*
Henry Holt® is a registered trademark of Macmillan Publishing Group, LLC
120 Broadway, New York, NY 10271
mackids.com

Library of Congress Cataloging-in-Publication Data
Names: Gilligan, Paul, author.
Title: King of the Mole People / Paul Gilligan.
Description: First edition. | New York : Christy Ottaviano Books, Henry Holt
  and Company, 2019. | Series: [Underbelly] | Summary: Seventh-grader Doug
  Underbelly strives to be a normal middle-schooler, but as secret King of
  the Mole People, weird things are attracted to him.
Identifiers: LCCN 2019003104 | ISBN 9781250171344 (hardcover)
Subjects: | CYAC: Middle schools—Fiction. | Schools—Fiction. | Kings,
  queens, rulers, etc.—Fiction. | Imaginary creatures—Fiction. | Humorous
  stories.
Classification: LCC PZ7.1.G555 Kin 2019 | DDC [Fic]—dc23
LC record available at https://lccn.loc.gov/2019003104

Our books may be purchased in bulk for promotional, educational, or business
use. Please contact your local bookseller or the Macmillan Corporate and
Premium Sales Department at (800) 221-7945 ext. 5442 or by email at
MacmillanSpecialMarkets@macmillan.com.

First edition, 2019

Printed in the United States of America by LSC Communications, Harrisonburg,
Virginia

10 9 8 7 6 5 4 3 2 1

For Eleni, Evan, and Rosa,
who I love from the bottom of the earth.

CONTENTS

CONTENTS

PROLOGUE

It's not fair. You do everything you can to be a normal, average kid.

You do sports (ugh). You eat normal, average things for lunch. You try to keep your clothes relatively free of mud and make sure you don't smell too much like mushrooms.

You get a small part in the school play, but somehow, through a series of suspicious events, you get stuck playing the lead role, which is way more than you bargained for. And you're standing on the stage, toe to toe with Becky Binkey, the most popular girl in the school, delivering your lines, and everybody's watching. And you start to fool yourself. You start to think, *Hey, maybe this isn't so bad. Maybe everybody is beginning to accept me as a normal kid after all. Maybe everything is going to turn out okay.*

And then a giant twenty-foot-long worm comes ripping through the floorboards, showering you in a wave of thick, wormy mucus.

So long, normal.

ME: DOUG UNDERBELLY

1

NORMAL

Wait. That wasn't a very normal place to start a story, was it?

I've been working really hard on this normal thing. It's pretty much become my whole focus in life. But it's turned out to be something I'm quite bad at. And I have no idea why, because I'm a completely normal kid.

But for some reason I have a hard time getting others to agree. Look, this is me in school trying to throw a note to my best friend, Simon. I'm faking a yawn and pretending to scratch my armpit as I launch the note because I need to get it way over to the other side of the room now that Miss Chips moved Simon as far away from me as possible.

Simon was part of my new plan to achieve normality. It was a bold plan, considering my old plan for normality was doing nothing. I was under the impression that the best way to be average was to just keep your head down and mouth shut and coast along in the middle. But nope. Turns out that just makes you sink to the bottom.

When I moved to this new school a few months ago I thought maybe I'd have a fresh chance at normalness. Nope again. The bottom has a distinct reek to it, and my Cross Creek Middle School classmates sniffed me out on day one. Somebody had already called me "Under-smelly" before I'd even reached my chair.

To make things worse, since our move to this new neighborhood there've been a number of additional uncooperative developments. The kind of developments that are decidedly unhelpful to a kid who has made "being normal" his primary goal. I don't know why, but weird things seem to be drawn to me. It's like weird things sense where other weird things already are and then just pile on, like some kind of snowball effect. Except something less pleasant than snow. A mud-ball effect. And let me tell you, it's no fun at the bottom. Everything lands on you.

So about a month ago, I decided that instead of continuing to do nothing, I was going to make some moves. I came up with a checklist of things that regular kids did: Talk. Belong to groups. Live in a regular-looking house. I recently heard it was normal for seventh graders to have crushes on girls, so I developed one of those. I picked Becky Binkey, the girl everyone else already has a crush on, just to be as normal as possible about that too.

And have a best friend. I picked Simon. He was a good choice because he was right around the mid-level I was aiming for. I was in no way looking for actual popularity. That would be like a caterpillar wanting to be an airplane. I just wanted to be, say, a moth. That's what Simon was—a plain, simple moth. He offered me a piece of gum one day and we've been best friends ever since.

BEST FRIENDS

DOUG
(NOT PASSING A NOTE)

SIMON

MUTUAL
INTERESTS:
• JOKES
• HATING SPORTS
• GUM

But Miss Chips had made Simon move to the other side of the room, which made me have to throw notes. Miss Chips had just finished giving us an assignment. We had to interview someone who we thought was "The Most Interesting Person You Know." Everyone grumbled because kids hate assignments, and I grumbled the loudest just to be even more normal than everyone else.

This was a "make-work" assignment, which is a term I'd picked up from Simon. Simon was a "Brainer," so liked to learn things. Miss Chips hated her job, so didn't like to teach things. She'd give us assignments like this one that didn't require any preparation on her part. Sometimes she even got us to mark each other's assignments so she didn't even have to do that, a system that was ripe for injustices. One of the Brainers asked who'd be marking things this time, and Miss Chips said she would. Ed yelled, "Then I pick you, Miss Chips!" and the class burst into laughs.

"I pick Principal Wiggins!" I shouted, but nobody laughed, even though it was the exact same joke. I can't stand Ed. Ed is a jock and he's super popular and all the girls love him. He's also my bully. I didn't have it on my checklist, but having a bully is another thing some regular kids have.

"Are you sure you don't want to pick your girlfriend, Magda?" Ted said to me, and the class erupted again. Ted is also a jock and super popular and all the girls love him. And he's my backup bully. I don't know how normal it is to have a backup bully, but Ted is almost a carbon copy of Ed, so if one of them is sick or something, I'm covered.

ED AND TED

SAWED APART AT BIRTH?

CLONED FROM THE SAME ORANGUTAN HAIR?

Being on the receiving end of a lot of jokes, I'd figured out one way to get more popular was to make people laugh. But it soon became clear that I'm not good at making jokes. So I got a joke book. I used to tell jokes from the book to Simon when he sat beside me, and he loved them, even though he wouldn't be able to laugh because he might get in trouble. He'd squirm uncomfortably without smiling and do a really good job of holding the laugh in.

Jokes that were made at someone else's expense seemed to get big reactions. So I scribbled one out on a piece of paper:

Then I crumpled it into a ball and did my fake-yawn-armpit-scratch thing and let it fly toward Simon. But I put so much effort into my theatrics that my aim was off, and it landed on the desk of Magda.

If you want to see someone who isn't normal, check out *Magda*. She always dresses in black and her hair looks like a melted package of licorice and her eyes are like two ping-pong balls floating in cups of oil. Her primary interests are talking to herself, and *ghosts*. She's the only person in the school who associating with would cause me to sink even lower. So of course she's always trying to talk to me. Like I said, weird things seem to find me. I'm not even going to risk drawing a picture of her.

Magda picked up the note and looked at me with her little ping-pong eyes and smiled. *Oh no*, I thought. *She thinks the note is for her!*

I pointed vigorously at Simon, and she made a "Wha—?" face, so I pointed more vigorously at Simon and she pointed at Becky

Binkey and mouthed the word "Her?" and then at Ed and mouthed "Him?" and then at several other kids. By the time I was jabbing my finger toward Simon like I was doing a shadow puppet of an angry woodpecker, I realized she was pranking me, and that I'd drawn the attention of my surrounding classmates.

"Geez, Underbelly, at least wait till after class to start interviewing your girlfriend," said Ed. Another eruption of laughs.

"She's not my girlfriend!" I shouted over the laughs. Lousy Ed. What I should have done was turn the comedic tables against him and said something like "Maybe she's *your* girlfriend!"

"Underbelly," said Miss Chips without looking up, and the laughter halted abruptly. Miss Chips had the world-weariness of someone who had been through several wars and the crustiness of someone who could have won them all single-handedly.

"Quit passing notes to your girlfriend," she droned, as if simply echoing fragments of things that had recently invaded her ears. Another round of laughs, which caused me to panic and respond defensively with the last thing I had teed up in my mouth: "Maybe she's *your* girlfriend!"—which didn't work at all. The laughs accelerated, but they were still aimed at me. Humor is like a soccer ball. It's hard to get it to go in the direction you want it to.

MISS CHIPS

SOULLESSNESS, POSSIBLY FROM NEVER HAVING A BEST FRIEND, POSSIBLY FROM WAR

CHIPS

"Magda," said Miss Chips, rubbing her temples. "Read what's on the paper." For someone who never lifted her head, she had pretty amazing perception.

Magda uncrumpled the paper. "Hmmm . . . seems to be a drawing of Ed and Ted . . ."

"What—?" I stammered. "Ed and—? It's not—"

"Yeah, it says it right here: 'Who's got four thumbs and four butts? Ed and Ted.' The implication being that their heads are also butts."

The class laughed a little, but it wasn't a pure laugh. It was more the laugh of a group of people about to witness something bad happening to someone whose welfare was of minimal consequence to them. There was a built-in problem with jokes that were at someone else's expense: they potentially caused manslaughter.

"That wasn't even meant for her, Miss Chips!" I said, my face now streaked with sweat. "It was meant for Simon! And I wouldn't have had to throw notes if you hadn't moved him to the other side of the room!"

Miss Chips seemed to suddenly remember she was in a classroom full of kids. "I didn't move anybody! But I'm going to move you to the roof if you cause any more disturbance! Now put that note in the trash!"

Dang creepy Magda! This was all her fault! Her ping-pong eyes glimmered at me as I took the note from her desk. I cast a look toward Simon as I headed to the trash can, but he slunk down in his chair, avoiding eye contact. Good play, Simon. No sense calling Miss Chips out on her lie about moving your seat away from mine and risk *both* of us getting in trouble because of our friendship and our love of jokes.

Ed and Ted glared at me as I passed. "Who's got two thumbs and one butt?" said Ed.

"That's about to be dangling from a goalpost?" said Ted.

I glumly pointed my thumbs at myself as I shuffled past. Could the day get any worse?

That's when I caught something out of the corner of my eye. A familiar shape, drawn on the outside of the window next to my desk. It was the shape of a crown. Drawn in mud.

I reached under the window with my shirtsleeve and smeared it away. Great. Now I was going to die with mud all over my shirt.

2

MUDDY

I thought maybe I was going to get detention for the note thing, but when the bell rang Miss Chips was the first one out of the classroom, so I guess she forgot.

Speaking of forgetting, Simon forgot to wait up for me at the door. His memory is pretty bad, since he forgets things like this a lot, which is surprising, since he's a Brainer and so has a really big brain. I was going to need his help to avoid Ed and Ted, who were no doubt using their tiny jock brains to figure out the best way to get my butt to the top of the goalposts.

I found Simon by the sign-up board.

"Simon! Hi! Want some gum? You gotta help me avoid Ed and Ted, they're looking to string me up!" Then I noticed the pen in his hand. "What are you signing up for? Is there a club about gum?"

"I offered you a piece of gum *one time*," he said. I read the paper he was signing.

"Rocket club! Oh, wow! That sounds like a blast! Ha ha! Get it?" I said, reaching for his pen.

"Are you sure you want to sign up? It's a science thing. It's sort of for people who are good at science."

"Great, that should keep out the jocks!" I said. "Man, I thought it was detention time for sure back there. What's the deal with Miss Chips lying about moving you away from me? What does she think? Two best buds are going to just move apart for no reason?"

Simon dropped the pen I was trying to take from him and bent to pick it up.

"Boys! We need boys!" came some girls' voices from behind us, which is a phrase that tended to sail unheeded over the head of someone like me. "We're desperate!" they added, which is a phrase I tended to give more attention.

It was Becky Binkey and her crew, and they were trying to get boys to sign up for the school play. I guess there were only so many roles that could be played by Marco. Marco has orangey skin and Elvis Presley hair and was once in a commercial for curly fries.

MARCO

ELVIS HAIR (WITHOUT THE SIDEBURNS)

SKIN TANNER FROM A BOTTLE

HOW HE PRONOUNCES "THEATER"

THEA-TAH

Another of the items on my normal checklist was trying to get accepted into a group. There were four groups in Cross Creek Middle School: the Jocks, the Brainers, the Artsies, and the Trendies. I know in movies they show more cliques than that, but we were only in seventh grade, so we kept it simple.

There was also that other item on my checklist about having a crush on a girl. Having the crush was pointless if nobody knew about it, so I thought this would be a good time to announce to the world that I, completely normal Doug Underbelly, had developed a fresh, searing-hot crush on the most poplar girl in school. But of course that's not something you just want to blurt out. I decided to start with something a little more subtle.

"I have a crush on Becky Binkey," I blurted.

I didn't have much experience with crushes.

Becky looked at me the way she might look if she'd just been spoken to by a tree. Then she looked like she was processing how one might respond to a talking tree. Fortunately for her, popular girls don't have to make those kinds of decisions. Her squad of "Binkettes" jumped in.

They all laughed heartily. Jokes at someone else's expense weren't as perilous if you traveled in packs.

I decided to take charge using the power of comedy. "Why do cows wear bells? Because their horns don't work!" Laughs, from me, at my own joke. I held up my hand. "High-five, Simon! Don't leave me hanging!"

But Simon wasn't there anymore. He must have gone ahead to scout for Ed and Ted.

Becky and the Binkettes had returned to their task of trying to get boys to sign up for the school play and were chasing after some down the hall, leaving me alone with the sign-up sheets. I signed up for the school play. And rocket club. And soccer (I got a bit carried away). I don't know if I was exactly "accepted" in any groups yet, but no one could deny I was on the lists.

By the time I got outside, the schoolyard was starting to clear out. I ran to the slide where I could wipe the mud off my shirtsleeve on the ladder and scan the area. No sign of Simon, but I could see Ed, standing guard at the front exit as students filed past him. Great.

I crouched down and realized I was standing on something. A familiar shape, dug into the ground at the base of the slide. It was the shape of a crown. Drawn in dirt.

I obliterated it quickly with my foot.

With Ed manning the front exit, I had no choice but to hightail it to the back. I hated to ditch my best friend like this, but there was no time to spare.

Of course Ted was guarding the back. Which should have been obvious. If you're a pair of clones, you can lock down a dual exit pretty handily.

I looked back and saw Ed heading my way. He must have spotted me. I was trapped! I looked across the field to the goalposts. I'd been hung by my underwear from fence posts and other lower-to-the-ground locations, but goalposts were a whole other level I couldn't bear to contemplate.

Then I saw something that wasn't there a minute ago: a tunnel, freshly dug, heading down under the fence that ran along the length of Cross Creek.

Why do I always have mud on me? This kind of thing right here was part of the reason. Because the truth is, when there are mysterious forces working on your behalf, sometimes you have no choice but to go along with it. Especially when there's a couple of Neanderthal jocks getting ready to turn you and your knickers into a waving flag.

I took the tunnel.

It was exactly my height, but it was slippery because it had been freshly dug. That's the kind of thing a normal kid doesn't know—freshly dug tunnels are slippery. Believe me, this is not information I wanted to possess. But for someone who did possess it, I was hoofing through that tunnel way too fast. As I sped toward the mouth at the other end I realized my feet weren't doing much of a job in the braking department. No job at all, in fact. The tunnel ran under the creek, and water was seeping into it, which was causing worms to start oozing out. I was already pretty out of control when I stepped on one.

Even more slippery than a freshly dug tunnel is a freshly dug tunnel filled with worms. And falling while running through a tunnel filled with wet worms turns the experience into a one-man luge.

WORM LUGE

WORMS (EQUALLY FRIGHTENED)

GOLD MEDALIST

When I sat up, dripping with mud and worms, I could see Ed and Ted glaring at me from the other side of the fence right near the spot where there was no longer a tunnel. They couldn't ask how I'd managed to get to the other side of a fence and a creek so quickly without admitting that they couldn't climb a fence and swim across a creek as fast as a puny non-jock like me. So they skipped the question and went straight to insults.

Again with the ten-foot pole.

And then they hit my sore spot.

"You're so *weird*!"

"I'm not weird!" I yelled. "*You're* weird! I'm totally *normal*! I've got a best friend! And I tell jokes! And I eat bologna sandwiches for lunch! *Normal!*"

And that's when I saw, out of the corner of my eye, the familiar shape again. Crowns! Dug into the grass beside the sidewalk, running all the way up the street. Over and over and over and over and over. And I *lost it*.

"Okay! All right! I get the message!" I bellowed to the sky. "I'm coming, *okay?* Sound the stone trumpets! Roll out the mud carpet! *I'm on my way!*"

Which—and this doesn't need saying—is not the best way to convince others that you're not weird.

I jumped up and ran down the street, veering left onto a cul-de-sac. All I wanted to do was get home and eat some normal food and maybe watch TV and relax. And at least I had a nice little house to do that in, which looks like this:

APPLE TREE

WHITE PICKET FENCE

PIE COOLING ON THE WINDOWSILL (YOU CAN ALMOST SMELL IT)

It's about as normal a house as you can get. And I live there.

Or that's what I tell everybody.

In truth, that's the house I walk up to, and that's the apple tree I hide behind while I make sure nobody's looking, and that's the picket fence I hop before sneaking up to my real house. Which looks like this:

BUILT IN THE TIME OF CHOLERA

ALWAYS DARK, NO MATTER WHAT TIME OF DAY

BATS (CAN YOU BELIEVE IT?)

APPLE TREES? WHO KNOWS, THEY'RE DEAD.

TOMBSTONES (YOU HEARD ME)

Wondering why I'm a little sensitive about being normal? This house is exhibit A.

My dad inherited it from some old relative, who was an undertaker. Dad's finances were categorized as "troubled," so we had no choice but to move in here. It's supposed to be temporary while he fixes it up to sell it, but that hasn't happened yet due to a bunch of lawyer words that were complicated but also meant "troubled." That and the fact that it's surrounded by graves, a number of which are lying open waiting to receive dead bodies. "Grave holes" is not an item you want to see on a real estate feature sheet. Ever since we moved here I've been spending hours after school cleaning up dead trees, scrubbing bat poop, and filling open holes. But the place seemed to resist any efforts at improvement. Bats poop a lot. And one grave hole in particular just wouldn't fill in no matter how much dirt I scooped into it.

Another thing that didn't help was the smell of boiled eel. Ingredients had already become unorthodox in our kitchen over the years due to that troubled-finances thing, and Dad, to his credit, had developed a real knack for innovative recipes. But when we moved here to Dreadsville Manor (my nickname for our house), we found a stream near the back of the property filled with eels (yup), and lo, they'd become the star attraction of our meals. Eel fillets, eel burgers, eel tacos, you name it. I'd been campaigning heavily to have them taken off the menu as not suitable for children, and after hundreds of hours of complaining I was finally making some progress.

The front door creaked like a sinking ship as I entered. I dumped my backpack and slumped against the wall, inhaling a deep noseful of Dad's latest eel concoction. Abnormal as it was, it was still home. And at least I'd managed to keep it a secret from the other kids.

"Hi, Underbelly," said Magda.

"WHAT ON EARTH ARE *YOU* DOING HERE??" I shrieked.

Magda. The one classmate who even minor contact with was social devastation. Right there in our very own hallway.

"I'm here to interview your dad for our 'Most Interesting Person You Know' project," she said, smiling.

"Wha—? My dad? He's not interesting! He's boring and normal! Perfectly normal!"

"Are you kidding? He's raising his family in a *graveyard*. And he knows how to make boiled eels!"

"But how did you know where I live?"

"Don't be ridiculous, Underbelly. Everybody knows where you live."

"Your school chum Magda says she loves eel!" called my dad enthusiastically from the kitchen. "So maybe you don't know everything, Mr. Eel-Isn't-for-Children! I invited her to stay for dinner!"

Magda smirked, her licorice hair dangling, her ping-pongs dancing in her cups of oil. Sigh, fine, since she insists on pushing herself into the story, *here*:

MAGDA

PING-PONG EYES →

LITTLE SMIRK LIKE SHE ALWAYS KNOWS SOME-THING

DEFINITELY <u>NOT</u> MY GIRLFRIEND

I slid past her down the hallway and up the stairs. I entered my room and locked the door. My checklist of normal was going right down the tubes. Normal house: *uncheck*. Crush on Becky: *uncheck*. Best friend: you may not have noticed, but that was hanging by a thread. The day was just determined to be terrible, so I figured I might as well continue with the unpleasantness and get the other chore over with as well.

I pulled a heavy garbage bag from the

back of my closet, slid open the window, and climbed down the tree to the ground. I dragged the bag through the decaying tombstones overrun with weeds and up a small hill to an open grave. I reached into the bag and pulled out a tall stone crown, put it on my head, and jumped in.

It's really, really tough to be a normal, average kid while also being King of the Mole People.

3

UNDERGROUND

The moment I dropped into the hole two things were waiting for me. One was a huge mud puddle. And the other was Oog.

Oog is a Mole Person. One of my "Royal Guards." And seeing me land splat in a puddle of mud caused him to burst into laughter. You might think the comedy value of someone falling in mud would have worn off for Mole People, but you'd be wrong. Mole People have a terrible sense of humor.

In case you don't know what a Mole Person looks like (and why would you?), this is one here:

OOG

TOAD-LIKE SKIN

PRACTICALLY NONEXISTENT EYES

HUGE HANDS FOR DIGGING

HUGE MOUTH FOR LAUGHING AT UNFUNNY THINGS

After getting hold of his laughter Oog remembered that I'm his King, and he dropped on his knees to grovel and praise my name.

"All hail King Doug!" said Oog.

"Okay, I'm here!" I growled. "I got the message! All fifty of them! So here I am! Your king!"

"King have bad day?" said Oog, back on his feet.

"As a matter of fact, King did have a bad day! Not a single thing went right! And this crown is so heavy it's crushing the bones in my neck!"

"Ha ha ha!" laughed Oog.

"What's funny about that?" I demanded.

"Sorry. Oog remembering when King fall in mud."

I told him I knew the deal: I see a crown symbol, I come to the Mole throne. I didn't need crowns drawn all over creation! "In case you forgot, I'm trying to keep this Mole King business hush-hush up there!" I said. "What's the big idea with the tunnel?"

"Uhh, Oog only draw crowns. Boogo make tunnel."

"Boooooog!" said Boogo, appearing from the shadows. Boogo had larger hands and a smoother body that aided his role as Master Digger, and from what I could gather he was really into gardening, which in the Mole world consisted mainly of tending to roots. I couldn't tell much from him, though. Most Moles seemed to speak English—or "Up-speak," as they called it—on some level, and Boogo understood it, but all he ever said was "Boog." He fell on his knees and groveled and (I'm guessing) praised.

"That's enough with the falling on the knees!" I said. "I already told you, it makes me very uncomfortable."

"King in bad mood," said Oog to Boogo.

"I'm not in a bad mood!" I yelled. "Isn't it supposed to be forbidden for Moles to let Up-worlders know of your existence? Well, what do you think they're going to say if they start seeing tunnels appearing and disappearing?"

Oog whispered something to Boogo and pointed at the mud puddle I'd fallen in earlier, and they both laughed.

"Why is that so funny??" I yelled. "You guys are covered in mud all the time!"

"Oog not know." Oog shrugged. "Somehow King do it funnier."

I didn't get why Mole People thought I was funny, but I'd have killed for laughs like these back in class.

"Look, can we just get on with this?" I said over the cracking of my neck bones. "It's been a rough day."

Oog came over to me. "Oog sorry. King tell Oog all about bad day King have in Up-world, and Oog listen. King not leave out details."

"There's no time for that!" said Ploogoo, appearing from the shadows. Mole People generally appeared from the shadows. Ploogoo was the third member of my Royal Guard. He looks pretty much the same as the other two, only more squished. There's not a whole lot of distinction between Mole People. Here are my three Royal Guards, with the differences pointed out:

Ploogoo was my head Royal Guard. You could tell because he had more Os in his name—in Mole culture, the more Os your name has, the higher your station. His command of the Up-speak language was better than Oog's, but he spoke quickly, as if the Up-speak disturbed his mouth, and constantly looked around like a kid who'd been made the lookout on a bank job that had started to go wrong. Despite being the head guard, Ploogoo seemed less respectful of my role as King than the other two. His fall to his knees and "All hail King Doug" were half-hearted and with no groveling whatsoever.

"You're needed in the Royal Court immediately!" said Ploogoo. "And stop asking about the Up-world, Guard-mole Oog. That's a violation of Mole law!"

"Ploogoo in bad mood," said Oog.

"I'm not in a bad mood!" said Ploogoo. "*Croogoolooth* is in a bad mood!" It seemed like bad moods were running rampant. Although to be honest, Croogoolooth was always in a bad mood. Croogoolooth was my Royal Advisor, which as you can tell by the number of Os in his name was a higher rank than my guards. He has six Os. Apparently the old king had sixteen. They wanted to start calling me King Dooooooooooooooooog, but I put a royal halt to that.

"King say crown hurt neck," said Oog.

"It sure does!" I agreed. "It weighs like fifty pounds!"

"The crown must be worn at all times while in the Mole world," said Ploogoo.

"But look at it, it's ridiculous! Why is it so tall when you all live in low-ceilinged tunnels? It keeps getting knocked off my head by stalactites!"

BONK!

← STALACTITE

ANOTHER THING NORMAL KIDS DON'T KNOW: THE DIFFERENCE BETWEEN STALACTITES AND STALAGMITES

"Insulting the crown is a violation of Mole law," said Ploogoo. Ploogoo was a real stickler for rules. This love of rules was probably what kept him supporting the crown despite his distaste for who was currently wearing it. "Now let's go. There are reports of unrest in the lower levels. Plus I already mentioned Croogoolooth's mood."

"I'm not going anywhere until I get my new throne pillow," I said.

If you assumed a Mole throne must be comfortable since it was built for a king, guess again. Almost everything in the Mole kingdom is constructed of only three materials: mud, roots, and rock. And also I'm pretty sure Mole People butts have a different anatomy than human butts, because even being made of rock didn't account for how utterly painful that throne was to sit on.

"Oog has new throne pillow for King!" said Oog proudly.

"You do?" I said.

"Oog made it Oog's-self!" he beamed (as much as a Mole Person can beam). "It waiting by entrance to Big Cavern!"

"The King is pleased!" I beamed back. "Okay, let's get this over with." I retrieved my crown, which had just been knocked off again by a stalactite. Ploogoo made some grumbling noises, and Boogo said "Boog," and we started down the tunnel.

It's surprisingly easy to see when you're in Mole tunnels. They don't have electricity (not advanced enough), or fire (nothing to burn), and Mole People themselves have terrible

eyesight. But they can see a bit, and they've coated all the tunnels in luminescent clay, so you can generally make out where you're going.

Oog moved up next to me as we hustled along and spoke quietly so Ploogoo couldn't hear. "TGIF!" He smiled.

"It's Tuesday," I said.

"To be honest, Oog not know what that mean. Oog overhear other Up-worlder say it while drinking big color drink through straw. He seem good mood."

"I thought you weren't supposed to be listening in on the Up-world," I said.

"Oog need listen in on other Up-worlders now King stop talking to Broom and Trout."

In case you're thinking I used to talk to a broom and a fish, you're wrong. But the truth isn't much less embarrassing. The fact is that while spending all those hours trying to fix up our backyard graveyard to make the place more sellable, I had a lot of time to think about my problems. So I started talking to the tombstones. I'd tell them about my day and complain about life on the bottom rung. The tombstones didn't judge me, and I guess it made me feel better remembering that some people had situations that made mine seem not so bad.

The two I talked to most were the ones that sat beside the grave hole that led to the Mole world (something I didn't know at the time) and belonged to Mr. Broom and Mrs. Trout. I'm not proud to say this, but they became kind of like friends.

Of course I wasn't aware at the time that my tombstone confessions weren't just between me, Broom, and Trout. The former King Zog (I'm going to dispense with the sixteen Os) started making a habit of listening in. And Oog joined him, developing quite a fixation on the sordid details of my existence.

Once I'd found out about the eavesdropping, I'd stopped. But I was missing having someone to confide in, and Oog was missing having a human to listen to. I checked to see that Ploogoo was a safe distance behind us, then started quietly telling Oog about my day, how every little thing in my life seemed bent on keeping me unpopular.

"King want be popular?" Oog quietly returned.

"Popular?" I snorted. "I'd be happy just not being the school bottom feeder. All the kids laugh at me."

"That not surprise! King have good sense of humor!"

"Falling in mud is not having a good sense of humor."

"Oog disagree. Humor all about timing."

"Yes," I said, "but there's a difference between everyone laughing at you and everyone laughing *with* you. Here, let me tell you a proper joke. Why do cows wear bells? Because their horns don't work!"

Oog didn't laugh.

"You probably don't know what a cow is," I said.

"No, Oog know what is cow. So this joke make someone popular in Up-world?"

"Well, not that joke specifically—"

"Oog!" yelled Ploogoo. "Up-world matters are not your concern! King Zog may have been loose with the Mole laws. But we're the Royal Guard. We have to set an example!"

"Part of Royal Guard job is to keep King happy," said Oog. "How we do that if we not learn about Up-world?"

"Have you not already learned your lesson from the royal scepter punishment?" said Ploogoo. "Have you not lost enough Os in your name?"

Oog gave me a sheepish grin. "TGIT," he whispered and pretended to drink from a straw, then gave me a friendly slap on the back.

SPLAT!

CROWN OFF AGAIN

The sound of the splat echoed through the tunnel and partially covered the dull rumbling that had been steadily growing louder. It's a rumbling sound unlike any rumbling sound you've ever heard. Like hundreds of walruses doing bad Frankenstein impressions with tubas stuck on their heads.

It was the sound of Mole People.

The tunnel opened up into a big cavern—which the Mole People unimaginatively called "the Big Cavern"—and it was filled with Mole People as far as the eye could see. To put that in perspective, even with all the luminescent clay, you couldn't really see that far. But even still, it was an impressive amount of Mole People.

The Moles closest to the entrance turned and squinted at me, then squinted some more, then fell on their knees with their arms stretched toward me, praising my name.

"No, stop it, don't—" I stammered.

With their terrible eyesight, any Moles beyond the first few rows were barely able to see

me. But Mole People are very group-minded, so if a few of them start doing something it ripples outward until all of them are doing it. This is a useful feature if you want to get Moles on one side of a room to react to what Moles on the other side of a room are seeing. It also means the entire population can change their mind about something surprisingly quick.

The groveling and praising rippled across the giant room until hundreds of Mole People were chanting "All hail King Doug," "Glory to the King," or just long, deep "Ooooog" noises from the ones with limited vocal ability. Mole People have guttural voices (even the females), and all of them chanting together created quite a stunning resonance directed toward me at the center. It was super, super embarrassing. But it was also quite a spectacle. Here was an entire society of beings, bowing down to me. Doug Underbelly. Their King.

I stepped forward, tripped on something heavy, and fell face-first into a mud puddle.

The sound of hundreds of Mole People

laughing is resonant too, but maybe not as stunningly.

"Now is not the time for comedy," said Ploogoo. "Royal Advisor Croogoolooth is waiting!"

"I tripped on something," I said through a mouthful of mud.

"Your new throne pillow!" said Oog. "Oog make it special!"

Oog lifted a small pillow. Which, of course, was made of rock. What was I expecting something in the Mole kingdom to be made out of? Then it slipped out of Oog's hands and landed on my spine with a loud THUMP! The Mole People's laughter resonated even louder.

Oog was right. Comedy was all about timing.

4

THE MOLE KINGDOM

Mole People have always had a fascination with the Up-world, and humans in particular. They've been listening in on us for ages, which is why they all speak Up-speak. But they've always been fearful of what humans might do if they learned Moles existed. So they came up with a bunch of Up-world laws:

1. Never let an Up-worlder see you.
2. Never take anything from the Up-world.
3. Never show interest in the Up-world.
4. If you're choking, raise your arms over your head.

I think the fourth law was misplaced from another list, but the third law had been growing more lax in the wake of the former King. King Zog had apparently been developing quite a human-positive attitude. Based on his research (eavesdropping on me while I was talking to tombstones), he found humans not scary or dangerous, but in fact meek and delightful and kind of funny, and had even gone so far as to suggest that humans and Mole People might get along. He'd come back with stories about humorous human rituals like getting hit with food during lunch or getting hung from fence posts by underwear. The Moles were captivated by these stories, and the Moles' positivity toward humans had run rampant. Case in point:

MOLE → CROWN

HUMAN ←

Between being a human and being their King, the Moles basically treated me like every celebrity in *Super Famous People Magazine* rolled into one. That is, if celebrities were showered with grubs.

Grubs were the Moles' main food source. There were grub gardens everywhere, and throwing grubs at someone was considered a form of respect. Grubs rained down on me so heavily I had to scrunch up my shirt collar and keep my lips pressed tight to keep any from landing in unwanted places.

The Mole rumblings grew so loud they shook dirt off the walls as the Royal Guard ushered me forward into the Big Cavern.

The cavern was about the size of a soccer field, but a lot less flat, and it had a big hole in the center that plunged deep into the bowels (ew) of the earth, which they of course called "the Big Hole." The surrounding walls were lined with caves where Moles lived, which had been recently decorated with imitations of human home items like stone mailboxes, slate

MOLE HOME

ROOT CLOTHESLINE (MOLES DON'T WEAR CLOTHES)

STONE MAILBOX (MOLES DON'T GET MAIL)

GRUE LAWN

GR MO

curtains, and clotheslines made of roots. Their front lawns were grub gardens, and some Moles had kept actual moles (like, the little ones that dig holes in your lawn) as pets, although for some reason a law was passed forbidding these.

As we made our way toward the throne the throng surrounded me, feeling my clothes, rubbing my sneakers. One of them held out a baby Mole and I kissed it. I'm pretty sure one chopped off a piece of my hair. Flat stones were thrust at me with calls of "Autograph!" and dozens of gravelly voices joined in, "Autograph! Autograph!" I always thought it was jerky when celebrities refused to sign autographs, so I did my best to oblige. I took the closest stone and hammer and chisel and began hammering away as the others jostled and held forth their own chisels and rocks.

"Enough!" a voice cut through the rumblings. The voice was a little on the squeaky side for a Mole Person. But there was a simmering down, somewhat, and the rain of grubs subsided.

Behind the Mole throng a worn ramp led up to the royal platform, and at the top— on what by Mole standards was a lush and comfortable-looking seat—sat Royal Advisor Croogoolooth.

Even though Mole People all sort of look the same, Croogoolooth somehow managed to look more unattractive than the others. Maybe it was the wide head, or the horns, or the skin that had the texture of crushed bugs. Or maybe it was his personality.

Mole People were generally roundish, which made it easier to move through tunnels. Croogoolooth had lots of angles. He didn't move easily through anything.

"Bring forth the 'King'!" he said without looking up. He always said "King" as if it were in quotes.

Ploogoo was as much a stickler for orders as he was for rules. "Step aside! King coming through! This way!" he called out as he nudged me throne-ward, my hammer and chisel clanking against the autograph stone.

Unlike the rest of the Moles, Croogoolooth had no fascination with humans. In fact he made it clear he despised us. He never bowed to me. Or looked at me. Or seemed to be able to stand breathing the same air as me. Which was strange considering he was the guy who had brought me down here to be King.

"Looks like our 'King' finally decided to join us," he said to the Moles as we reached the top of the platform. That's another thing he did, he never really spoke directly to me. Instead he just sort of announced things about me to the crowd.

He snatched the autograph I'd been working on, which contained only the tiniest of dents. "Look at this pathetic autograph!" he said, holding it up to the crowd. "These tiny pink hands can barely lift a chisel! They can barely hold the royal scepter!"

He tossed the royal scepter at me and I bobbled it a little but managed to grab on to it.

The royal scepter was not another item made of stone but was, in fact, the long-handled shovel I'd been using in our backyard that had gone missing six weeks ago. One evening I'd stepped on it and the handle flipped up and smashed me in the face. This wasn't the first time it had happened, and I got mad and threw it into the grave hole that never seemed to fill up. It had somehow made its way to the Big Cavern, and despite the law against Up-world possessions, King Zog had taken a liking to it and declared it his royal scepter.

After Zog's disappearance Croogoolooth found out that it was Oog—who was called Oogo at the time—who had brought the shovel down (in order to demonstrate the hilarious joke he'd seen the human do with it). Croogoolooth removed an O from his name as punishment. But it was too late to remove the shovel/scepter. The Moles had taken too much of a shine to it.

It was about a month ago that King Zog disappeared. Because they didn't know if he was dead or not, there was some delay in selecting their new king. They were all very fond of their human-friendly King and wanted to give him a chance to turn up.

During this time Oog continued to visit my grave hole, looking for Zog but also to keep listening in on my confessions to Mr. Broom and Mrs. Trout. The fact was the entire population of Moles had got caught up in the miserable soap opera of my life, and Oog kept everyone up-to-date with the latest reports. I had to believe the only reason they found my life compelling was because it was the only one they were currently following. How else could they be so enthralled by complaints about being picked last on the co-ed softball team and the difficulties of scraping bat poop off a Weedwacker?

But such was the interest in me that when, a few weeks later, the time came to finally select a new king, Croogoolooth got the bold idea to drag me down to be a contender.

The method Moles used for choosing their king was simple enough: put the crown on the head of each candidate and listen to the rumbling from the crowd. Whoever had the loudest rumbling kept the crown. I don't even know if I was up against anybody, or even how loud the rumblings were since all I could hear at that point was my own screaming. But the love of humans was at its max. And so I was declared King Dooooooooooooooooog.

Of course I refused immediately. I told them I was having a hard enough time trying to be normal above ground without anyone finding out I was the King of muddy, half-blind underground creatures. But Croogoolooth coldly informed me that the people had spoken, and that if I refused to report to the throne on my own they could simply open up a hole in the earth and suck me down in front of all the Up-worlders if that's what I preferred. So instead we came to a compromise: whenever they wanted me, a Royal Guard member would sneak up and leave a drawing of a crown where I could see it, and I would know my Kingliness was required. Sure, the Mole People had spoken, but I assumed if I just did the job badly enough, they'd eventually stop calling.

That was about two weeks ago. Long enough for me to develop a reputation at school for smelling like mushrooms, and for me to develop bruises on the bruises on my butt from the royal throne, which Croogoolooth was at that moment shoving me toward.

I may have had the crown on my head, but Croogoolooth sure acted like the one in charge. He'd been Royal Advisor to the last king, so I guess the Moles were used to his grumpiness. Or maybe I just thought that way about him because he was blackmailing me into being a Mole King.

"The 'King' will now take his seat," said Croogoolooth, helping me onto my throne.

SHOVE!

MOLE THRONE (SEE WHAT I'M TALKING ABOUT?)

The crowd erupted in cheers. My butt erupted in pain.

To make it even worse, the throne immediately began vibrating with the CLANK CLANK CLANK from the hammer of the Royal Artist, who was chiseling my likeness into a statue. I had to hand it to him, he was capturing my expression perfectly.

"Why? Why is the throne so painful?" I said.

"Insulting the Mole throne is a violation

of Mole law," whispered Ploogoo from his position behind me.

"But Croogoolooth's chair seems so—" I started before Croogoolooth cut me off.

"I, Royal Advisor Croogoolooth, the Unmuddied, Keeper of the Laws, ambassador to the lower realms, and holder of six Os in name, pronounce the Royal Mole Court to be in session."

Mole People eyes are kind of hard to see, but you could still make out that a lot of them were rolling at Croogoolooth. Unpopularity was something I was familiar with, and I recognized it on the Moles' faces whenever Croogoolooth spoke.

"The King will now hear issues presented by his subjects and put forth his royal rulings," said Croogoolooth, "which I'm sure will demonstrate a solid and thorough understanding of his people. Step forth the first plaintiff!"

The Moles clamored and eventually one stepped to the base of the ramp and spoke. "My King! Love you! Huge fan! So tell me, how are things going with your crush on that girl at school?"

"This isn't a forum for asking questions about the King's life!" said Croogoolooth. "It's for presenting problems so the King can make a proclamation and you can see what he's really like. Only come forward if you have a problem! Next plaintiff!"

A female Mole stepped forward. She looked kind of cute for a Mole, even with the huge horn sticking out of her forehead. "Yes, me have problem. Need King help. Problem is, me look for love in all wrong place. Will King marry me?"

The Moles all went "WoooOOOOoooo!" and started banging rocks together.

"That's not the kind of problem I'm talking about!" yelled Croogoolooth. Then he noticed the horn-headed Mole was holding a small actual mole with a bow made of roots stuck to its head, which she coddled like an old lady with a purse dog.

"You know pet moles are a violation of Mole law! Get rid of it immediately or I'll have it thrown down the Big Hole!"

The Mole People didn't like that much and began grumbling, but Croogoolooth yelled over them.

"The King is here to listen to disputes and dispense binding proclamations! I instruct you for the last time, restrict yourselves to putting forth issues which demand his royal decree!"

The next subject stepped forward. "What is 'Taco Tuesday'?"

"Okay, forget it, that's enough of the Kingly presiding," said Croogoolooth, to another chorus of grumbling. "We have pressing matters to attend to."

"I have a pressing matter," I said, and an expectant hush rippled across the chamber. "I, uh, I don't want any more kneeling and groveling. It makes me . . . uncomfortable."

"The King is uncomfortable!" called Croogoolooth. "He decrees no more kneeling and groveling! Anything else, 'Your Majesty'?"

"Uh, well, can we do something about this throne? It's really hurting my butt."

"The throne is hurting the King's butt!" announced Croogoolooth.

"Look, I've got a few tissues," I said, pulling them out of my pocket. "Maybe I can at least put them under my—"

"Up-stuff! Up-stuff!" the Moles started yelling. One of the tissues slipped from my hand and wafted over the Moles' heads. They started scrambling over each other trying to reach it. One made a successful lunge, and they all fell into a big pile, wrestling and grunting. They were really gaga for Up-stuff.

"Seems like the King cares more about his butt than the welfare of his people!" announced Croogoolooth. "There are rumblings from the lower realms! The Slug People are restless! And the Stone Goons are having problems with the Mushroom Folk! But I guess the King thinks he's too far above us to be concerned with such lowly matters!"

I didn't think I was above them. Well, not

figuratively. Literally I was. But the Mole People didn't have it so bad. Yes, they lived below us humans, but being on level two was actually pretty good. There's a whole bunch of levels below that. It looks something like this:

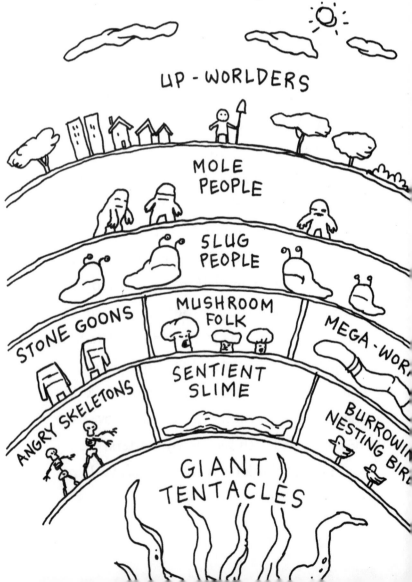

"If the Mole People continue to be threatened by the lower creatures, who knows how long it will be before we'll need to rise up and take over the surface world!" Croogoolooth said with the emphasis of a sports announcer.

"Take over the surface world?" Ploogoo said. "I can't imagine our people ever wanting something as extreme as that."

"They would," Croogoolooth said, "if Slug People were trying to take over *our* level!"

"Slugs?" I said. "Aren't slugs, like, the slowest and laziest things on the planet?"

"The King has a point," said Ploogoo. "The Slug People grumble a lot, but I doubt they have enough motivation to start a battle."

"So we should wait until motivation strikes?" said Croogoolooth. "Am I the only one who cares about keeping our kingdom safe and strong? Shouldn't that be the duty of the *King*?" He put his hands on his hips and looked out at the crowd, like this should have been some sort of cue, but the Moles just whistled and yahooed and threw more grubs.

"I'm sorry, everyone," I said, starting to feel a little bad about all my complaining in the face of such an adoring public. "It's just I had a really bad day. I got in trouble with my teacher. I had two bullies after me. And I got covered in worms."

A murmur went through the throng, and I heard them repeating the word "worms." Yeah, they understood. Worms are wriggly and slimy and super gross. That's something we could all agree on.

"You mean little worms, like this?" Croogoolooth peeled a worm off my shoulder. It must have been stuck there since I fell in the tunnel.

"Why didn't you tell me that was there?" I whispered to Oog.

"Oog thought King keep there on purpose," whispered Oog. "Like pet."

"This worm isn't big enough to hurt a grub," said Croogoolooth, holding it up for the masses to inspect.

"But there were dozens of them!" I said.

"Oog and Boogo dug an escape tunnel for me near a creek, and water leaked into it, which made it fill up with worms. You know how worms are with water, how it makes them crawl to the surface."

The word "surface" seemed to be a trigger word for Croogoolooth. "Why would we know that?" he roared. "We don't get to be on the surface! We're stuck here, on the under-level, while you Up-worlders bang around above us with your loud machines and big drills and stompy-stompy parades!"

"Try being stuck at the bottom of seventh grade," I mumbled.

"The King is now blaming his Royal Guard for not keeping him happy enough to focus on his duties!" announced Croogoolooth.

This caused a bunch of noise from the Moles that was hard to decipher.

"If I could just bring down a pillow from the Up-world," I said. "A single pillow. That's all I ask. And maybe a soda. All the water around here is fifty percent mud."

"Oog make pillow," said Oog, holding up the rock.

"No, Oog," said Croogoolooth. "Our King is too good for Mole pillows. Let him bring a pillow from the Up-world. And maybe a soda."

"Up-stuff is strictly forbidden!" said Ploogoo.

"If the King wishes to change the law about bringing down Up-stuff, so be it!" said Croogoolooth. "Let the word ring out! King Doug has decreed that it is now acceptable to bring Up-stuff from the Up-world!"

The Big Cavern erupted with huge rumblings of joy. I hadn't really said that I wanted to change the whole law. All I wanted was a pillow and a soda. And from what I'd witnessed, Moles didn't deal well with possessions, especially Up-stuff. But everyone seemed happy, which helped me in my more immediate goal of getting the heck out of there.

I peeled my butt off the throne and replaced the royal scepter in its holding spot, and the Royal Guard surrounded me and ushered me back through the crowd toward the cave mouth. The throng hooted happily and I tossed the remaining tissues into the crowd to tumultuous cheers. It was nice to feel liked.

"If only I could please the Up-worlders in my life so easily," I said to Oog as we entered the tunnels that led back to the grave hole behind my house.

"It job of Royal Guard to keep King ready to do his King stuff," said Oog. "If Up-worlders not see how great King is, Oog fix."

I didn't know what Oog meant by "fix." But it was a pleasant change having someone be interested in making things better for me instead of worse. In hindsight I should have paid more attention.

5

THREE EPIC FAILS

The next morning I sat at the breakfast table staring directly at my dad. This was because my neck was so sore from wearing the fifty-pound crown that I could barely turn my head, but he mistook it for interest in what he was saying. Which it was not. Because he was talking about Magda. About her love of ghosts. About her questions for him for our class project. About ghosts again.

"She's so unique," he said. "Just like you."

"Unique is bad," I informed my clueless father. "When are you going to understand that?"

"And she loved all my eel dishes. Especially

the eel pudding I made for dessert. I bet you're sorry you missed out."

By the time I'd returned from Mole duty last night it was already dark. After confirming that Magda had left and my dad was busy with boiling pots on the stove, I took a bath to get off all the dirt and grubs, which, as usual, clogged the bathtub drain. By the time I'd got it unclogged with a plunger and a long-handled screwdriver (grubs really jam up in there) I was tired and in no mood for whatever food was left over, so I dragged myself to bed.

"But fear not," said Dad, following me to the front door with my lunch bag. "I packed some for you!"

"Dad, I told you I need to eat normal things for lunch! It's hard enough for me at school without eel stew and eel nuggets and eel pudding. I need to eat *sandwiches* like normal kids!"

"I *did* make you a sandwich!"

"Is it an eel sandwich?"

Dad held out my lunch with a frozen smile.

HUGE
TEETH
AND TOO MANY
OF THEM

DAD

EEL
DRIPPINGS

I loved my dad. But he was undeniably weird. And we inherited this house from a weird relative. So I guess weird runs in our blood. Which isn't exactly great for me and my quest to not be weird.

"How much longer are we going to live in this place?" I said. "I thought we were only here until we could sell it! I'm out there working my butt off making the graveyard look as good as a graveyard can look! Did you know that you can get bat poop off concrete with dishwashing soap? *A normal boy shouldn't know that!*"

"Well, there are some legal issues which the lawyers described as 'troubled,'" said Dad. "Troubled" again. Maybe there *weren't* any more complicated lawyer words. "Troubled" seemed to cover it. "But don't worry, I've got some ideas! Big ideas!"

"Are they about eels?" I asked.

Dad's smile was starting to cake in the corners. He gave the lunch bag a little shake. I snatched the bag and slammed the door.

Imagine my father thinking that being unique was something positive. Here I was busting my butt trying to fit in, trying to overcome these monumental hurdles like living in a graveyard, eating primarily eel, and having a father who had more than a passing resemblance to an old portrait you might see in some show about a haunted mansion. I was drowning in uniqueness.

But at least nobody knew my deepest, darkest secret.

"I know your secret, Doug Underbelly," said a creepy voice.

I turned my head sharply and my neck cracked so loud a bunch of birds flew off from a tree. But I needn't have bothered looking. I knew the voice of my licorice-haired classmate, which somehow had the audio equivalent of bits of eggshells in your eggs.

"I learned all sorts of interesting things from your dad last night," Magda said.

"You haven't learned anything," I said with confidence, "other than maybe how to puree an eel."

"Oh, really?" she said with that knowing smirk I couldn't stand. "Well, I know you disappear into the backyard graveyard and don't come back for hours."

"So what? Maybe I like talking to tomb-stones," I said, attempting to use the truth as a smoke screen.

"Your dad's concerned about you, Underbelly. I told him not to be. That I'm keeping an eye on you. And that I'm going to help you with the job I know you're doing."

The twinkles in her eyes started to make me sweat. *What if she did really know? It would be all over for me! How on earth would I ever be normal if she tells everybody that I'm—*

"Communing with ghosts!" she said.

Oh, thank the stars. "There's no such thing as ghosts. Now, if you don't mind, I'm on my way to school."

She walked behind me as I snuck through the long grass and dead bushes in my yard toward the white picket fence of the sweet little house next door. Magda may have figured out I lived in Dreadsville Manor, but I had to cling to the hope that she wasn't telling the truth about everybody else knowing it too.

"Why would you pretend to live in a boring house that looks like it's from a Precious Moments figurine when you actually live in an awesome one?" she said.

"Because my house is embarrassing and weird. Of course, you'd probably love it."

"I would totally love it," she said. "Weird is great. You should embrace it."

"*I'm not weird!*"

"You literally have a grub on your back."

It's really hard climbing over a fence when you can't move your neck properly because of all the squished bones and you're trying to hurry because you're trapped in a conversation you're dying to get out of. Too bad I was already halfway over when I noticed the section of fence beside me was missing (!).

"Why are weird things always drawn to me?" I moaned as my shorts got caught on the fence top.

"Maybe it's like cats," said Magda. "You know how they always crawl all over people who don't like them? Maybe it's like that with you and weird things."

"So are you saying if I liked weird things, they wouldn't be drawn to me anymore? Well, that's great."

"Stop thinking in terms of weird or not weird, and just start being yourself. Seriously, rocket club? Acting? *Soccer?*"

"So now you're spying on me?"

"Yeah, I do it all the time," she said with pride. "That's how I know you talk to ghosts. Ghosts named Broom and Trout."

"Stay out of my backyard! In fact, stay away from me entirely! The last thing I need right now is another 'weirdness zone'!"

With a ripping sound my shorts came free of the fence and I landed hard on the other side. You may have noticed the title of this chapter indicates "Three Epic Fails." This wasn't one of them, since there was nobody there to see it.

"Epic fail, Underbelly," said Magda. Nobody that counted, anyway.

The Three Epic Fails happened at school over the next week, one in each of the three groups I'd joined in an attempt to fit in better, not worse.

Entering Cross Creek Middle School was not vastly different from entering the Mole world. The hallways threaded like tunnels through the school, popping out into classrooms where teachers rumbled and grumbled. And instead of shaking dirt from the walls, the roar from the cafeteria shook lockers in the adjacent hallways.

Once you entered the cafeteria you had to be on constant guard for racing students and flying objects. It was a huge room with posters lining the walls informing you that "You are what you eat" (great for someone with eel juice dripping from their bag) and listing rules for everyone to ignore about staying in your seat, being quiet, and not making a mess—posters ironically obscured by dried lunch ingredients.

The teachers had long ago given up enforcing any rules and spent their monitor duty chatting about anything that was unrelated to kids. If Miss Chips was on duty, she'd sit staring downward the whole time unless one of the flying objects hit her, at which time the kids nearest to her would freeze, and a silence would ripple out over the room like a wave while everyone waited to see if Miss Chips would respond or not.

Within these lunch-encrusted walls the groups butted up against each other, overlapping, retracting, spitting members into and out of themselves. It was no place for the fainthearted. A free agent like me didn't stand much of a chance.

Especially with the added peril of being seen with Magda, who insisted on sitting wherever I sat. On several occasions I didn't eat fast enough and the kids started a ritual where they would draw a ring around our table, which they dubbed the "weirdness zone," and into which they would pile all their garbage. Magda would yell at them and throw it back out, taking ownership of the circle as if it were

a space she had created for us on purpose.

I soon decided it was safer to eat my lunch in an unused alcove behind a bunch of dusty old boxes of Brillo pads from a misguided school fund-raiser.

Hiding in alcoves was a good way to keep the crowd from spotting eel sandwiches, though it did nothing to help with joining groups. But I had high hopes my sign-ups were going to help with that.

Epic Fail One: Rocket Club

Over the next week there were gatherings of each of the three groups. The first was rocket club, which was held in the science portable classroom, which you could find because of the big sign on it that said SCIENCE. For some reason the sign was missing, so my first brain test was to figure out which portable was the science one by going to all the wrong portables first. I guess I was the only one who hadn't already been to the portable lots of times, since I was the only one who was late.

The problem with trying to fit in with Brainers is that it's hard to pretend you're a Brainer if you're not. My plan was to stick close to Simon and agree with whatever anyone else said, especially if it sounded smart. I'd also learned a few big words that I was going to try to slip in. And gum. Give everyone gum.

I found my new rocket-mates (eventually) preparing rockets and trying to come up with a name for the rocket team. Suggestions included "the Newtons," "the Kinetic Kings," and "the Launch Lords." I snuck up behind Simon and offered my idea.

My rocket-mates looked at me. "Are you sure you want to be here?" said one.

"Oh, yes!" I said. "I love rockets! They're totally quadrennial. Right, Simon?"

Simon dropped his pen again and bent to pick it up. The other Brainers accused me of not knowing what that word meant, or even how to spell it. I pointed out that it was a very difficult word to spell, so not knowing how to spell it was no proof that I didn't know what it meant. So they asked me to spell "wick."

"Uhh . . . W . . . H—"

They tossed me out of the club. But that wasn't the Epic Fail. The Epic Fail was that as I was heading toward the door something tripped me, almost like a piece of the portable floor suddenly poked up under my foot. I fell headfirst into a bunch of beakers full of garishly colored, bizarre-smelling chemicals.

I could hear the laughs of the rocket club as I stumbled away. I hadn't got to use my second big word ("avuncular"). But I still had two more groups to offer gum to.

Epic Fail Two: Tryouts for the School Play

The problem with trying to get a part in a play is that it's hard to pretend you can act if you can't. The only acting experience I had was pretending to yawn and scratch my armpit at the same time. But I had a trick prepared. I'd watched a famous scene from an old black-and-white movie that they always show as an example of someone who was doing a really great job of acting, and I'd committed it to memory.

I found my new theater-mates on the auditorium stage, stretching and doing vocal warm-ups. Miss Chips had been put in charge of the play by Principal Wiggins, and she was not happy about it. Somehow she managed to be even less involved than she was during regular class. But it didn't matter, since everything had been taken over by Becky Binkey and her Binkettes.

I was hoping the Binkettes had failed to recruit any boys besides Marco, but there were a number of other boys, including some pretty popular ones. I'd been clinging to the fact that at the sign-up board they'd said "desperate," though there's no way I was going to tell them that.

Becky stood at center stage staring at a clipboard and surrounded by Binkettes. Marco stood nearby wearing a scarf, even though we were indoors, repeatedly flipping an end of it over his shoulder with an air of confidence that indicated he already had the lead wrapped up, which he did. I envied his ability to display confidence. But I didn't have a scarf. All I had was a joke book.

Marco stopped flipping his scarf, and the Binkettes took a moment from gossiping about boys and clothes to wrinkle their noses at the source of the interruption and then tell me I stunk worse than normal. (It had been a few days since the chemical spill, but I still hadn't been able to scrub away the smell.) Marco gave the standard line about a ten-foot pole. One of the bolder Binkettes reached behind my ear and flicked a grub onto the ground (come on, seriously?) and then asked me what I was even doing there.

"You said 'desperate,'" I said. *Dang it, Underbelly.*

"All right, let's get started," said Becky, crossing the stage with a clipboard and using some kind of sixth sense to step around the dead grub on the floor. People like Becky never had any gross things happen to them, even completely by chance. "Who wants to go first?"

I saw my big opportunity and took it. I jumped to center stage with my famous scene at the ready. Everybody looked at me (except Miss Chips, who had started to snore). I dug deep, deep inside myself, and into the heart of the black-and-white movie hooligan whose acting I'd memorized, and gave it everything I had.

"Hey, has anyone seen the spotlights?" said one of the Binkettes. "They seem to be missing."

Everyone had stopped looking at me. Becky passed by with her clipboard and handed me a Post-it Note. I guess I was supposed to be transported somewhat by the flutter of her hair or the smell of her pink lemonade lip gloss, but I didn't know if the crush was still on or not. There was no gentle brush of our fingers during the note pass.

It almost seemed like the note left her hand a split second before it touched mine, so that if weirdness were like electricity and a Post-it Note was a conductor, she'd be safe from getting zapped.

I looked at the note.

A part! I got a part! I didn't care if it was small! In fact, small was perfect! There's no way anything embarrassing can happen if your part is a shrub!

Cue the second Epic Fail.

Something caused the floorboards beneath me to suddenly jut upward.

I was starting to think maybe I'd imagined it happening in the science portable, but this time there was no mistaking it. I fell into the backdrop, knocking it loose and sending the entire set crashing down on top of me.

This was immediately followed by something even more unsettling. Miss Chips looked at me.

A hush fell over the room. When someone who never looks at you suddenly makes eye contact, it's extremely impactful. Even from across the room her eyes bore into mine like a laser beam and sent shivers through my spine. Then a final piece of the set fell on my head, breaking the laser beam and making it safe for my classmates to make noise again. The acoustics of the room really deepened their full, hearty laughs.

I'd forgotten all about the gum, but it seemed like a better idea to take the opportunity to sneak away under cover of the destroyed set. Nobody'd said anything about taking my part away because of the accident—but then I'd never really given them a chance—so I didn't know if I could count this as a victory or not.

But there was still one more shot at group-joining awaiting, and despite the fact that it was sports, I was strangely hopeful. Surely lightning couldn't strike three times.

Epic Fail Three: Soccer

Signing up for soccer seemed somewhat ludicrous, not only because of my lack of any physical skill, but also because the soccer field was the stomping ground of my two bullies. So I was pretty surprised when I made the team. I guess that's an advantage of having bullies who aren't that bright—they're easily distracted. Either that or their interest in hanging me from goalposts was outweighed by their interest in having a properly hydrated team.

Water is a lot heavier than it looks. Coach Parker—who was basically a grown-up version

WATER BOY!

COUNTS AS PART OF TEAM!

SOCCER VERY THIRSTY SPORT

ARMS LONGER ← BY END OF GAME THAN AT START

of Ed and Ted—insisted I keep dumping out perfectly good water and hauling fresh jugs from the school just to make sure the temperature was always nicely chilled. I overheard Ed and Ted discussing whether it would be okay for both of them to pick Coach Parker for the "Most Interesting Person" assignment, even though his only point of interest was his ability to be constantly sweating from the head.

Liking water didn't prevent Ed and Ted and the rest of my team—the Cross Creek Crickets—from treating me the same as before. They complained about the water temperature, questioned how it was possible that I was muddier than they were, and told me to stop offering them gum.

But the end of the practice was nearing, and I'd managed to get through without messing anything up. Well, a couple of water jugs went missing, and so did a couple of the players' bikes, but I couldn't be held responsible for that. I was a member of the team, and I felt great!

And then, alas, the final Epic Fail. For the third time—and by now there could be no mistaking the pattern—something protruded from the ground at an inopportune moment and sent me crashing into something loud. This time it was into the stack of water jugs, which collapsed painfully on top of me, the final one popping its cork and drenching my head.

Once again there was laughter—my teammates, the coach, even an old lady who was passing by. And so help me, I almost *ordered* everyone to stop laughing. For a moment I'd forgotten where I was. Belowground I was King of the Mole People, but aboveground I was just king of slapstick.

It's just like I told Oog—there's a difference between everyone laughing at you and everyone laughing *with* you. If he didn't believe me he should have seen *this*. He'd have *loved* it.

And that's when it hit me. These were no accidents! This was *Mole humor*! *This* is what Oog meant by "fix"!

And then there it was, my old friend Mr. Crown, freshly drawn in the mud.

Ughh! You crazy Moles! You thought causing me to crash into a bunch of things was going to make people like me? Well, guess what, you needn't have bothered with the stupid crown drawing, because you were already about to get a visit from your very furious King!

6

GIANT SLUG

I was so irate I almost didn't stop for the crown before heading down the Mole hole, but it had been made clear to me that nothing I said mattered if I wasn't wearing the crown. I jammed it onto my head, warning Mr. Broom and Mrs. Trout as I passed that if they felt the ground rumbling below them not to worry, it was only the King of the Mole People down there raising heck.

It became evident there'd been some changes in the Mole kingdom in the week since I'd been there last when a car tire rolled past me down the tunnel.

As I neared the Big Cavern the Mole

rumbling was louder than ever and punctuated with sounds never before heard in the lower realm. A cacophony of clangs, whirs, bells, and blares . . . and also lots of angry complaining. Mole People were generally jolly, so the sounds of anger seemed out of place.

As bad as it sounded, it was nothing compared to the way it looked. The cavern was piled from stalagmites to stalactites with Up-stuff. I noted things that had recently gone missing in the Up-world, like stage lights, bikes, water jugs, a section of white picket

MAILBOX

PENCIL SHARPENER

GOALIE PAD

fence, and a big sign that said SCIENCE. There was practically anything you could name. Although none of it was being used correctly.

As I began pushing my way through the mob I couldn't help but notice the absence of praising and groveling, which was as it should have been after my order to stop doing it. But there was also an absence of woo-hooing and autograph seeking, and not a single grub flew my way. All of my subjects' attention was devoted to their new possessions. Some were enjoying themselves, but many were distressed by their confusion over how things worked or were fighting over items like big, muddy toddlers.

I found Croogoolooth resting in his comfortable chair at the top of the royal platform, surveying the scene with a look of accomplishment.

"What's with all the stuff?" I yelled to him over the noise.

Croogoolooth just pointed at the list of Mole rules on the wall. Number two—*Never take anything from the Up-world*—had been chiseled out. Oh right, that law I supposedly changed.

Royal Guardsman Ploogoo was helping the Mole with the forehead horn cover a basket with a bunch of blankets when he spotted me and rushed over. Unlike Croogoolooth, he displayed no satisfaction whatsoever.

"What's the deal with all the pranks, Ploogoo?" I said, remembering my raising-heck objective. "I was falling all over the place up there! Everyone was laughing their butts off!"

"Well, I'm glad Your Majesty was having fun," said Ploogoo. "Your latest decree has caused lots of fun down here as well, as you can observe."

"I can observe that everyone is using everything wrong. Teapots are not shoes. And fishing poles are not Q-tips—"

"The King has not been summoned to be an instruction manual," said Croogoolooth. "A dignitary from the lower levels has been requesting an audience. In fact, he seems determined not to slither away until he gets one." This last part he said with extra disdain on top of the regular amount of disdain Croogoolooth poured onto everything.

But my mind had latched on to the word "slither."

"The Royal Mole Court recognizes . . . *the ambassador of the Slug People!*"

The "people" part of "Slug People" is misleading. There is no "people" part of them. They're really just huge slugs with slightly more face than regular slugs. They have beady eyeballs that sit on the end of stalks above their huge, cavernous mouths on the quivering, gelatinous mounds of their gooey white bodies. Wrapped in a sash, if they happen to be an ambassador.

SLUG AMBASSADOR

SLIME

SLIME

SLIME

"Nice of you to make time for me, Croogy," said the Slug. "We don't get up here much."

That was true. The Slug People resided one level down from the Moles, but the Moles and Slugs seemed to have an arrangement similar to the Moles and humans—keep to your own level. Sometimes Slugs would bristle at being treated as lower-class simply because they were lower, and sometimes they'd make threats about taking over the Mole level for political leverage or because one of the even lower groups was threatening the Slugs. Things that are on the bottom tend to try to move up. And everybody listens in on the level above them, as was made clear by the fact that the Slug also spoke Up-speak.

Croogoolooth talked about Slug People with the same contempt as Up-worlders. So it was strange that Croogoolooth had granted him an audience. And even stranger that he'd allowed him to get away with calling him "Croogy."

"Slug Ambassador, may I introduce you to our new 'King,'" said Croogoolooth, tossing the royal scepter at me and shoving me down onto the throne, causing me to screech painfully. The place was crammed with Up-stuff, and I'd forgotten a pillow.

The Slug looked me up and down. "This is your king? What, you guys lose a bet?" And then he belched. Yet another thing normal kids don't know: giant Slugs belch a lot.

"Disparaging our King is a punishable offense!" said Ploogoo.

"Heh, only kiddin' around," said the Slug. "He just ain't easy on the eye-stalks, is all. How'd such a scrawny human get to be your King anyway? He'd never make it through the Great Slugging."

"Great Slugging?" I said, scrunching my nose up at the waft of Slug belch that had just hit my face.

"Yeah! When it's time to choose a Slug King we all pile on top of each other and then try to climb to the top while crushing the other Slugs below us into pulp. We call it the Great Slugging. Why, how do you guys do it, Croogy?"

"Never mind," said Croogoolooth.

The ambassador then started asking about the old King, how he could have just disappeared, how strange it was that nobody had found a body or anything. He was asking these questions in a general way, but was pointing them more toward Croogoolooth, who seemed to be squirming a little.

"How awful that he just vanished," said the Slug. "Well, awful for the old King, I guess. Maybe not so awful for anyone looking to take his place . . ."

At that moment Oog and Boogo clamored onto the throne area, covered in fresh mud and beaming proudly. Oog was wearing a soccer jersey, but upside down like a skirt, and Boogo wore a potted plant on his head like a hat.

"Well?" said Oog. "What King think?"

"There you are!" I yelled. "What's the big idea making me fall down all over the place?"

"King like? King so funny!" laughed Oog.

"Sometimes things that disappeared turn

up again unexpectedly," said the Slug, as if part of a different conversation.

"Everyone was laughing at me! Those water kegs flattened me like a pancake!" I yelled.

"Ha! King have such great comic timing. Now King be more popular in Up-world!" said Oog.

"Like if someone made a deal to get rid of a certain something," said the Slug, "but then someone didn't keep their side of the deal, and that certain something suddenly—"

"Oh really?" I said. "If I'm so popular why did I get kicked out of the rocket club or get stuck hauling water for the soccer team?"

"Hey, I'm trying to make a point here!" yelled the Slug. "There's some subtext involved!"

"All right, Ambassador," said Croogoolooth, "you've had your audience with the new King. Shouldn't you be oozing off?"

"Yeah, I gotta get going myself—" I started.

"Wait, Oog get King this!" said Oog while shoving an Up-world pillow under my royal heinie. The instant relief was almost heavenly.

BUTT PILLOW HEAVEN

SLIPPING SLIGHTLY INTO A COMA

"And also this," said Oog with a wave, and Boogo stepped forth and dropped a soda machine down. Oog took a soda from the machine, popped the top, and handed it to me. "No more mud water for King."

The Moles near the front started banging on the soda machine, trying to get a soda. A can popped out and they fell onto each other, growling and clamoring for it. The one who got it didn't know how it worked and bit the side, causing soda to spew into the faces of the surrounding Moles.

"You Moles are always insulting us Slugs," said the ambassador, "but your new King has turned this place into a gong show!"

"Hey, King Doug be awesome King!" said Oog forcefully. "Plus he hilarious!"

"Really? He doesn't seem that hilarious," said the Slug. "And it doesn't sound very kingly to schlep water or get booted outta clubs. In fact, it sounds pretty embarrassing."

"The ambassador's right . . . ," said Ploogoo.

"Our King shouldn't be getting treated like he's at the bottom . . ."

"Well, it's impossible to get any higher with all the popular kids in the way . . ." I mumbled, coming out of my butt-pillow coma.

At that moment there was a huge CRASH as a structure a bunch of Moles had been building out of couches and cement birdbaths collapsed, and Moles started fighting each other for the cushions and broken bits of pedestals.

"The King's new decree about Up-stuff is turning our domain into chaos!" announced my Royal Advisor.

"I don't know if I really said that, Croogy," I said, taking a long swig of my soda.

If I thought "surface" was a trigger word for my Royal Advisor, it was nothing compared to "Croogy." He turned and stared straight at me. Once again, when someone who has made a point of never looking at you suddenly makes eye contact, it's extremely impactful, and even more so if the eyes belong to a super-irate Mole Person with extremely sour grub breath.

Although he was inches from my face, he continued to talk as if making announcements to the masses. "The King didn't take into account his subjects' current ill-advised fascination with the Up-world! Or their tendency to get carried away with things!" And then he paused, as if to give emphasis to his final sentence. "It's like he doesn't know his people at all!"

He wasn't wrong. I didn't really know Mole People. I barely knew human people.

I think my spine was still supporting me upright on the throne, but internally I felt like I'd melted into a puddle. I could barely formulate words. "I guess . . . if I did change the law . . . it was a mistake?"

"Let the royal proclamation ring out!" yelled Croogy (let's face it, "Croogy" was just a lot easier on the tongue). He broke eye contact and turned to the crowd. "The King has decreed that all items taken from the Up-world are now forbidden!"

I was sure I hadn't said that either, but all I could concentrate on at that moment was the excruciating task of getting my eyelids to blink again.

"All Up-stuff must immediately be *thrown down the Big Hole!*"

A huge rumble of Mole dissent filled the cavern. Croogy snatched the soda from my hand and pillow from my butt and tossed them down the hole, and then started grabbing things from other Moles and firing them down the hole as well. "Don't blame me. Kingly order. Your human king decreed this." The Mole rumbling shook the walls.

"Moles seem angry," said Oog.

"People don't like being forced to give up things that are dear to them," said Ploogoo, spotting something or someone and leaping into the crowd.

He wasn't kidding. My butt was now in twice as much pain as it was before.

Under Croogy's commands the disgruntled Moles began dragging Up-stuff to the hole and lobbing it into the abyss. When you saw all of it funneling together it was a surprising amount of material. I wondered where the hole led to.

For a second I thought I heard Boogo going "Boooog," but when I looked at him he was unenthusiastically hauling the soda machine toward the hole. Then I realized I was getting *booed*.

"Dumping unwanted things down holes again, huh?" said the Slug, trying to make himself heard over the item-dragging and Mole-rumbling. "That's what you Moles do! Well, just remember, some things don't stay down holes! Do you hear me, Croogy? *I said, do you hear me, Croogy??*"

"Wait!" I said, jumping off the throne. "I need those water jugs!"

The Slug released a monstrous angry belch and then began oozing away. Watching a slug move is a weird, slimy sight at the best of times. But watching one "storm off" is even more freaky. Then one of his eye-stalks swiveled back at me, and he said:

It was a pretty scary threat, especially coming from a giant Slug, but I was busy dragging the water jugs and a stage light toward the exit tunnel. I saw Oog and Ploogoo talking and glancing my way. Oog smiled and waved, and I yelled out, "No more fixing things!" but I couldn't make my voice heard over the Mole noise, and Oog gave me a big thumbs-up.

A collective croak of Mole sorrow filled the cavern as Boogo managed to push the soda machine over the lip of the Big Hole and it disappeared into the darkness.

It sure was a bizarre experience being King of the Mole People. But what I was about to experience next was even more outlandish.

7

POPULARITY

As I mentioned earlier, I was never aiming for popular. All I wanted was to somehow claw my way up the ladder to a comfortable middle rung. Popularity was way too dangerous territory. And after my week of Epic Fails, it wasn't territory I felt I had any reason to worry about. But then the disappearances started happening.

Things began about a week later when Simon came up to me and offered me a piece of gum. I said yes, even though I had loads of it. Then I cracked a joke that I'd made up myself, and Simon laughed.

Simon told me Miss Chips had always been bitter but that she'd gotten extra bitter after the fund-raiser she'd organized to sell Brillo pads had failed so miserably. That explained all the boxes in my secret lunch alcove.

He then told me that for some reason members of the rocket club kept failing to show up for rocket meets, and there was a minimum number of "Accelerators" (the team name they came up with) required for the team to enter rocket shoot-outs.

At first I didn't get what Simon was asking

and thought maybe he wanted me to schlep water for the Accelerators, or rocket juice, or whatever it was that made rockets go. But it turned out the rocket club actually wanted to have me back on the team!

There were a number of important test launchings over the coming weeks, and I did everything I could to make sure I fit in with the Brainers and didn't blow it, starting by learning how to spell "wick." I took important-looking books out of the library and made sure to carry them around with the spines showing. I also sewed elbow patches onto a jacket and tried to inject any smart-sounding knowledge I had into conversations wherever possible.

PROFESSOR DOUG

STALACTITES ARE THE ONES THAT COME FROM THE TOP.

THERE ARE 10,000 KNOWN TYPES OF MUSHROOMS.

DID YOU KNOW THAT SLUGS BURP?

I was part of the Brainer crew, even if it was by default. And even though I did end up becoming a sort of rocket club equivalent of a water boy (rockets are heavier than they look too), Simon and I were swapping gum again, and I was fitting in just a bit, and I was doing it all on my own without any so-called "fixes" from my Royal Guard.

While arriving at a rocket meet a few days later I ran into Magda. Her ping-pong eyes zeroed in on my elbow patches and one of the books I was carrying that turned out to be in Latin.

"How's that 'just be yourself' advice I gave you going?" she said, pulling at one of my elbow patches and revealing my shoddy sewing job.

I explained to her once again how being seen with her was harmful to my goals, especially with things starting to work out for me. But like the cat that won't stop crawling all over the person that hates cats, she wouldn't leave me alone.

"I found out something really cool, Underbelly!" She beamed. "About a couple of friends of yours!"

This was immediately suspect, as I didn't have "a couple of friends." She handed me some printouts. I caught the name "Benjamin Broom" on one and "Eleanor Trout" on another. My "ghost buddies," as she called them.

"I looked them up online! Check it out: Benjamin Broom, died June 22, 1944. He was the owner of a pickle company. And he died working late one night by drowning in a vat of pickle brine! And here: Mrs. Eleanor Trout, died April 3, 1959. She was impaled by a moose! Did she ever say anything about a moose when you were talking to her?"

"How many times do I have to tell you? There's no such thing as ghosts," I said, pushing past her, stopping only to pick up my elbow patch, which had now fallen off completely. "Now, if you'll excuse me, I've got rockets to accelerate."

"*Sic semper explodius*," she called after me. "That's Latin for 'Don't blow your hands off.'"

There was more good news at the school play. Due to some of the other boys not showing up for rehearsals, they were being kicked out of the play by Miss Chips. Miss Chips was more interested in punishments than she was in the ramifications of punishments. Becky Binkey was left scrambling trying to fill the other boys' roles, and it was decided that a shrub wasn't as necessary as the speaking parts, so I got bumped up!

At first I became a shopkeeper with a couple of lines about "that Johnny Boy," and then I became the Mayor, who passes a law against dancing because of "that Johnny Boy," and then I became that Johnny Boy's impish best friend who actually dances with one of the Binkettes. The only boy part left was Johnny Boy himself, who has stolen the heart of the mayor's daughter, which of course was being played by Marco.

Marco clearly resented my rise up the ranks. He thought acting parts should be granted due to talent and not attendance, and he sniffed his nose regularly after my line deliveries. And the Binkette I had to dance with managed to maintain a fifty-fifty ratio of theater smile and icky face the whole time we were in contact. This was the kind of dangerous territory I was talking about. Nobody sniffed their nose or made icky faces at me when I was a shrub.

But as much as I was starting to sweat, I was undeniably and deeply embedded in a group, and I did everything I could to fit in and not blow it. I looked up the word "thespian," and I got a scarf and a beret and started talking with what I thought sounded like a British accent.

Then things went that one step too far. Marco didn't show up for a rehearsal. And Miss Chips canned him.

Becky begged her not to, but punishments were the only thing that gave Miss Chips any hint of pleasure, so Marco was out. Becky stared at me, obviously processing what this meant for her, since she was the mayor's daughter.

I was in a daze as I left the rehearsal, but then I started to wonder if maybe this was one of those things where the universe only gives you what you can handle. Maybe I was ready for this. Maybe it would be okay.

I was exiting the school, giving my beret a jaunty adjustment, when I ran into Magda. Well, I didn't run into her. She was sitting on a half-wall drawing something in a notebook and she started yelling "Underbelly! Underbelly!" louder and louder until I started running the other way, but she leapt off the wall and started chasing me, yelling "I saw one, Underbelly! I saw one of your ghosts!"

No one who hated cats ever got this much attention from cats.

"I saw it heading into your backyard!" she said breathlessly. "Maybe it was Mrs. Trout, out hunting for the moose who impaled her! It was too far away to see any antler wounds. It barely even looked human. Its shape was something like this!"

EYES TOO BIG

HANDS TOO SMALL

OTHERWISE UNCOMFORTABLY ACCURATE

Well, that was another Mole law broken.

"Maybe it was Mr. Broom!" continued Magda. "Do you think pickle brine melts features if you soak in it long enough?"

"I'd like to ask you a serious question," I said. "Do you think, if a person is trying to prove he's normal, that having someone run across the schoolyard yelling to him that she's seen a ghost is beneficial, or not beneficial?"

She burrowed her ping-pongs into my scarf and beret as if she hadn't noticed them until that moment. "You seem to be doing well with the school play."

"It just so happens the theater group has taken a fancy in me talents for their jolly-good show."

"Berets are French, not British."

Whatever. I was in too good a mood to let some potshot about European fashion bring me down. The theater group needed me, even if again only by default. And once more it had nothing to do with any "help" from those law-flouting Moles. All those things

I'd been doing to try to fit in, and it turns out the most important thing is simply showing up! If other kids were going to keep missing things and paving the way for me, it was fine by me. I was the lead in the school play! How "embarrassing" was their King now?

I flipped the scarf over my shoulder a little too hard and it swung around my head and slapped me in the eyes. My eyes were watering so much I couldn't locate the school exit till Magda gave my shoulders a twist in the right direction.

The biggest shock of all, however, was waiting for me on the soccer field. I was schlepping water bottles as usual when Ted approached me. It was so weird to see him without Ed, I hardly recognized him.

I thought maybe he'd finally decided to forgo the ten-foot pole and follow through on the plan to hang me from the goalposts. But instead he asked me if I wanted to join the team! Like, properly on the team, as in on the field where the ball gets kicked. A number of Cross Creek Crickets had been failing to show up (including Ed!), and they needed at least six players, so I was told to get on the field!

I was so discombobulated at first that I went on the field with a water jug and almost got kicked out of the game. Once that was sorted out I spent most of my time running around trying to make it look like I was after the ball when in fact I was trying to make sure it never came near me. Keeping away from a ball is harder than it looks.

But I was accepted into yet another group! I was ecstatic! Even the fact that my outdoor-sports debut coincided with record-breaking amounts of rainfall couldn't burst my bubble. I'd grown somewhat accustomed to mud. I got a headband and a pair of those running shoes that you pump up with a little air pump, and I started using terms I didn't really understand.

And then something even more amazing happened.

It was about a week later during the game against the Cross Creek Crickets' archrivals, the Baron Hill Bandits. The score was tied and we were near the end of the "second half" (soccer term). I was working my shorts off avoiding the ball, as usual. But a soccer ball is like humor: it's hard to predict where it's going to go. And without me realizing it, the ball was suddenly right at my feet.

With opponents converging on me, I panicked and hoofed the ball randomly. And that's when the amazing thing happened.

The ball was headed out of bounds. But then it curved around in a long, slow arc and headed toward the net. A couple of opposing players tried to intercept it, and the ball dodged and swerved around them, leaving them kicking air. It was like the ball was being guided along by the very ground beneath it. I must have accidentally put some crazy spin on that kick!

The opposing goalie rushed forward for the save, and the ball bounced up over his head and into the net.

GOAL!!!

My team went wild! They didn't pick me up and carry me on their shoulders or anything like I've seen them do in movies, but they did gather around me and pat my back and say "crazy shot." I was the hero of the game!

Afterward it started pouring rain again, and I overheard some people saying they couldn't find some things, like umbrellas, and coolers, and the playground slide. But the way I was feeling, nothing was going to burst my bubble. Not even a drawing of a crown. It was half washed away by rain, so I decided to pretend I didn't see it.

The three familiar voices coming from a storm drain were more difficult to ignore.

I peered into the drain at my Royal Guard, who looked like they were on just as much of a high as I was. I couldn't guess why. It's not like *they'd* just scored a winning goal.

"Did King see how we score winning goal?" yelled Oog. *Dang it!*

"So you guys did that, huh?" I said, accepting the truth. I guess what difference did it make—the ball either went in because of an amazingly fluky spin, or because of amazingly weird underground digging by a bunch of Moles. Who cared which? It was one of the best moments of my life. "Thanks."

"We wait whole game for King to finally kick ball!" said Oog.

"It's true. It's almost like Your Majesty was trying to *avoid* the ball," said Ploogoo.

"As if! Would someone who wears shoes like *these* avoid soccer balls?" I said, starting to pump up my shoes.

Being part of the King-building activity with Oog and Boogo seemed to have loosened Ploogoo up. He was smiling and making lighthearted remarks, and the Up-speak didn't seem to bother his mouth so much.

"Did you see the look on the goalie's face when the ball went over his head?" laughed Ploogoo.

"It was pretty funny. He was like,

wooooooo-aaat??" I said, making an exaggerated face, and we all laughed.

"Same as look on kids who fall in holes!" laughed Oog.

And POP went my bubble.

I'd heard the rumors of course. Kids were claiming the reason they'd been absent from wherever they were supposed to be was that they'd fallen into holes. Holes they swore weren't there a second before and that they couldn't climb out of, until a bit later when it was too late to make it to whatever thing they were supposed to be at, and then suddenly the hole would seem to get a little shallower and they could manage to climb out. But the stories seemed so ludicrous that everyone figured it was just kids making far-fetched excuses for cutting out on things.

I guess it seemed slightly less ludicrous to me, but I also guess I just didn't really want to think about it.

"So, you guys dug those holes that kids fell into?" I said with resignation.

"It easy when you got Master Digger!" said Oog, slapping Boogo on the back.

"Boooog!" said Boogo.

"No more getting kicked out of clubs or carrying heavy water for our King!" said Ploogoo. "Although we couldn't help notice you were still hauling jugs."

"Coach Parker said that even though I'm a player now I still had to be water boy since we didn't have anyone else to do it."

"Coach Parker, you say . . ." said Ploogoo, and whispered something to Boogo.

"Look, guys, I really appreciate your help, but I don't want you trapping any more kids in holes. I can handle things myself from here on. And besides, you gotta watch yourselves. Someone spotted one of you in my backyard!"

"King mean Dark Eyes? Oog see her talking to King a lot," said Oog in a singsongy voice. "She King's girlfriend?"

I forgot I was still pumping my shoe, and it exploded.

"She's not my girlfriend!" I said.

"She seem nice girl. Why King not like?"

"I don't not like. She just gets in the way of my plan! Her and her ping-pong eyes . . . licorice hair . . ."

"We have a saying in Mole culture," said Ploogoo. "It roughly translates as, 'You protest too much.'" And they all laughed.

"What about you, Ploogoo?" I said. "I've seen you chatting with the Mole with the huge horn on her forehead. Maybe she's *your* girlfriend?"

"She's not my girlfriend!" said Ploogoo.

"Ploogoo protest too much!" said Oog, and we all laughed again, including Ploogoo. But then he remembered his role.

"Has Your Majesty seen the crown symbol? We need you down here immediately."

"Let me guess, Croogy is in a bad mood?" I said.

"Actually, he seems to be in a slightly better mood. Which is surprising, since the place is filling up with Up-stuff again."

"What? I thought I put a stop to that!" I said.

It seemed my last decree merely forced Moles to get rid of all the previous Up-stuff. It didn't say anything preventing Moles from getting more. Moles are incredibly literal. As soon as the last of the old Up-stuff was chucked down the Big Hole, the Moles just started getting new stuff and then fighting over it even worse than the first time.

"Moles not deal well with possessions," said Oog.

"Yeah, so I noticed," I said. "But why

didn't Croogy tell me that? Y'know, for a 'Royal Advisor' he doesn't exactly advise me much." *I should start saying "Royal Advisor" like it's in quotes too,* I thought.

"Also, for some reason, the water isn't running off like it usually does," said Ploogoo. "It's getting really wet down here."

"Well, there's been a lot of rain lately," I said. "Speaking of which, I gotta go change out of these drenched clothes."

"Please try to come down soon, Your Majesty," said Ploogoo. "I'm not entirely sure what's going on. But there are some problems brewing that need your personal attention."

"Yeah, okay. See ya," I said, and they shouted goodbyes after me as I splashed away with my broken shoe.

Sigh. Didn't they know I was a kid with a lot in the works now? Between being an Accelerator, Johnny Boy, and a Cross Creek Cricket, I was swamped! "With great popularity comes great responsibilities" . . . or whatever that phrase was. Besides, with this much popularity, maybe I didn't even need to worry about getting outted as the Mole King, and I could just forget all about the stupid crown.

It did sound like there was some trouble happening down there in the Mole Kingdom. And it did seem that Croogy caused more problems than he solved, and was, in fact, kind of obviously a jerk. And I wondered if Moles maybe had some sort of personality blindness when it came to assessing the character of other Moles.

But on the other hand, why the heck did they need some seventh-grade human like me so badly? They'd been doing fine on their own until now. This wasn't the first time there'd been a bunch of rain. And sooner or later they'd figure out that the human stuff wasn't good for them and get rid of it. And that Croogy was a creep and demote him or something.

At any rate, I was way too busy with my own stuff now. They were just going to have to figure it out for themselves. I was done jumping through hoops trying to keep secrets hidden.

I looked over at the Precious Moments house as I neared home. Maybe I didn't need to bother pretending I was living there. I doubted anybody was watching anyway.

"Geez, Magda, do you sit here for hours waiting for me or what?"

She ignored the question. "Those kids that said they fell in holes! They weren't lying, Underbelly! They *really did fall in holes*!"

"How do you know?"

"Because, you know that ghost I told you I saw in your backyard? Well, earlier today I saw another one near the back of school property! It disappeared into the ground before I could get a closer look, but then I heard someone calling for help and I found a hole with Ed stuck in it! Do you know what that means?"

"Ed can actually survive more than five minutes apart from Ted?"

"It means these guys aren't ghosts! They can move material substances! And if they're going into the ground it's not because they're returning to their buried bodies, it means that's where they *live*!"

She was tenacious, I had to give her that.

"That's too bad," I said. "If it was Mr. Broom's ghost we could have got his pickle recipe and made a fortune."

She laughed. "And if it was Mrs. Trout's ghost we could have helped her find the killer moose that impaled her!"

"You could have helped her with a police sketch, judging from your ghost drawings."

"You're not bad yourself, judging from your Ed-and-Ted-monkey-butts art."

We smiled at each other. And the rain let up for a moment.

"So you haven't seen any of these guys?" she said, getting back to her point. "Come on, Underbelly! This could be some kind of incredible new species! Who knows, if we get credit for being the ones who discover them, maybe our names will be associated with them forever!"

I told her I had to go and pushed past her, trying to avoid the worms that had bubbled up from the ground in the rain.

"Wait! I know you're in a rush to go re-sew your elbow patches on your hoodie, but check this out! While I was in your backyard last week getting the dates for Broom and Trout, guess what I found?"

Gee, what could it be? I thought. *My bat-poop-encrusted Weedwacker?* No, it was something much worse. She reached behind a dead bush and pulled out the Mole King crown.

HOLDING IT ALOFT LIKE THE BABY LION KING →

"What's that gross thing?" I said, trying to act like I couldn't care less.

"I thought it was just a piece of one of the tombstones, but that was before I found out there might be creatures living under the ground. Now I think maybe it belongs to them!"

If you only knew who it really belonged to, I thought. The last time I returned from the Moles—a few weeks ago after the Slug Ambassador meeting—I was so weighed down with the water jugs and spotlights I'd saved from being thrown down the Big Hole that

I just dropped the crown by the grave hole. I guess I'd forgotten about it.

"Doesn't it look like some kind of weird crown?" said Magda.

"Looks like garbage to me," I snorted.

"Really? So you don't mind if I keep it?"

"Not at all."

"You don't need it for any reason?"

"Turn it the other way. I think it's a plant holder."

"It's so heavy. You mind if I try it on?"

"If you're sure you want to," I said. "But take a moment, because once you do you'll have crossed the line into being someone who puts plant holders on her head."

She smirked. "You've already crossed the line into being someone who sews elbow patches onto a hoodie."

I smirked back. But as she lifted the crown to her head, I had the strangest feeling of apprehension. Like the time I'd put out all my old toys at a yard sale, including this Hot Wheels car that I hadn't cared about in years but had once been my favorite. When someone picked it up, I felt a wave of protectiveness, like even though I didn't want it, that Hot Wheels just wasn't going to feel right with somebody else.

But what could I say to Magda? All I could do was watch as she slowly lowered the crown toward her licorice-haired head.

"Underbelly!" a voice called out, and it immediately started raining again. I had an impulse to leap into some bushes, but the bushes on my property were all of the prickly, poisonous, or dead variety. Besides, it was too late. I turned to see Ed, and Marco, and a bunch of other kids from my school. Mostly kids who'd lost spots in groups they'd joined. Or another way to say it—mostly kids who'd fallen into holes.

It was weird to see members of different groups all working together, unified against a common target.

"Pardon me," I said, taking a step toward the picket-fence house, "just on my way home."

STILL MUD ON HIM

ALONG TO SUPPORT ED

DRAMATIC LOOK LIKE HE'S TRYING TO MAKE MY HEAD EXPLODE USING MIND POWER

"Save it, creepo," said Ed. "Everyone knows you live in this creep house!"

This was a disaster. Caught out front of Dreadsville Manor with Magda. At least she wasn't wearing a Mole crown/plant holder on her head. But it's not like it mattered much. The way the two of us looked, we deserved ten "weirdness zones."

But they hadn't come for that. They'd come because of the holes. It had dawned on them that these holes had caused problems for a lot of kids, but there was only one kid who seemed to be benefiting from them. And it was the very kid who was often associated with *mud.*

"So we're going to finally get around to giving you that punishment!" said Ed.

"Perfect time, since the rain will wash off any of the mud and stink and grubs we get on us from touching you!" said Ted.

"Leave him alone!" yelled Magda. You could tell she was angry by the way her ping-pong eyes vibrated.

RUNNING MASCARA

MOLE CROWN/ UPSIDE-DOWN PLANT HOLDER

DRAWING OF GHOST

EXP SH

"Looks like your girlfriend wants to stand up for you!" said Marco.

"Mr. and Mrs. Creepo!" said one of the Brainers I didn't really know.

"Underbelly didn't have anything to do with those holes!" said Magda.

Uh-oh.

"For your information, they were dug by creatures that come from below the earth!"

No! Don't say that!

"And live in Underbelly's backyard!"

This immediately drew the attention away from me and onto Magda, and there was a general consensus that she was just as much of a weirdo freak as I was. And then I heard my voice saying things.

"At least she's unique! At least she's being true to herself, not like some carbon-copy jocks like you! Or some scarf-wearing theater snob like you! At least she's not boring like all of you are! Because being yourself is the only thing that really matters!"

I don't know where that all came from.

And I don't think I believed any of it. Even before what came next.

"She's not unique!" said Ed and Ted. "She's as fake as anybody! She dresses like she's some kind of vampire, but she lives in a house that looks straight out of a fairy tale!"

"Acting goth, talking about ghosts, it's just a bunch of cliché, run-of-the-mill rebelliousness," said Marco. "How typical. How 'normal.'"

"What?" I turned to her. "You live in the Precious Moments house?" Well, that explained why she was always able to spot me coming and going. "Why didn't you tell me?"

"It's embarrassing," she said.

"You're the one who told me to be real! Not to hide things!" I shouted.

"That's because you try to hide all the unique things that are cool!" she shouted back.

"There are no unique things that are cool! Everything weird that gets drawn to me just makes my life worse!" I turned to my lynch mob. "She's lying! She made all that up! There are no underground creatures! You know her, she's *crazy*! Always making up creepy stuff! I don't even know her! You can't choose your neighbors, am I right?"

I could tell I was not winning over the crowd.

"*I'm Johnny Boy! I'm an Accelerator! I'm a Cricket! I carry the rockets! I scored a winning goal! I'm totally normal now!*"

At that moment my dad opened the door. And there he stood, looking as much like a haunted house portrait as ever, holding a tray and smiling with enough teeth that he'd have fit right in on a poster for crocodile dentistry.

"Hello, Douglas," he said. "I thought I'd bring out a little snack for you and your friends. Hi, Magda!"

Then the rain faucet in the sky got cranked up to max, and even though everyone was already as wet as they could get, it became difficult to see and speak and presumably hang someone by their underwear, so my mob ran off. I accidentally looked at Magda and got nailed with her ping-pong-eye death stare before we each splashed up the walkways to the homes we were convinced didn't suit us.

8

WORM

I awoke the next morning clinging to hope.

By now it was impossible to deny that whatever social advancements I'd achieved had happened only because higher-level kids had got knocked out of the way. But even if what I had wasn't technically popularity, it was close enough for me. And I didn't want to alter a single thing that might destroy it.

With a night's sleep between me and the disaster in the front yard, I could almost convince myself that things might be okay, that maybe that little incident would be isolated, that maybe the heavy rain would wash away all the dirt. I still had my places in the groups.

The Moles had got me this far by digging holes. I'd told them to stop. I was ready to take it from here.

Since I'd just scored the winning goal over the Bandits, I figured I'd at least be accepted at morning soccer practice. I put on my headband and taped up my exploded shoe and ran downstairs to tuck into a hearty breakfast.

HUGE PILE OF LEFTOVER EEL S'MORES

I couldn't deny they were pretty darn tasty. Dad really did have a knack in the kitchen. (I wondered sometimes what he might accomplish with an egg.)

There was no Magda run-in at the foot of my walkway that day. In case you were wondering, yes, I felt a bit bad for trying to sacrifice her to save myself. But she's the one who burned me with her big be-true-to-yourself manifesto, which turned out to be a pack of lies. Besides, I didn't have time for anything else at that moment, I was in desperate goal-salvage mode.

I ran through the rain toward school while trying to pretend not to see the crowns drawn in multiple places along the way, or the fact that they were actually the "emergency crown" signal, which was the same as the regular crown symbol but with lines shooting out of it.

It wasn't until I was standing by myself on the soccer field in the drizzling rain that I realized soccer practice was obviously canceled.

Well, that was fine, I cared more about

being on the team than actually playing. And plus it gave me extra time to prepare for the rocket club meeting later.

There was nobody at the science portable either, so I changed out of my soggy soccer clothes and started stuffing rockets into a box so they'd be easier for me to schlep outside. As I was leaving I ran into Simon and he told me the rocket meeting was also canceled. In fact, everything was canceled. He'd come to make sure nobody touched the rockets, saying they were all delicately calibrated. I assured him that nobody had touched them as I blocked his path into the portable.

I asked why everything was getting canceled, and he told me that apparently Coach Parker had fallen into one of those holes that other kids had been saying they fell into. Now the teachers were taking it more seriously. All kids were supposed to report to the auditorium and stay there until the authorities could investigate.

I knew immediately what had happened.

I'd said "no more trapping *kids* in holes." Moles are incredibly literal.

By the time we got to the auditorium it was full, and the kids were being as loud and unruly as . . . well, an auditorium full of kids.

When some of the kids saw me they started pointing and making comments. I told myself that perhaps this pointing and commenting was because I was the star of the school play, or because I had scored the winning goal in soccer. But this seemed unlikely. Then I heard snippets like "Under-smelly" and "Probably dug all those holes" and "Eats eel for lunch," and that clinched it.

I found myself looking into the crowd for some kind of support and caught sight of Magda near the back, but her eyes were locked on the stage, her knowing smile pressed flat.

It didn't take long before the unruliness of the kids escalated to a frenzy, and it was clear it was just going to get worse. I was starting to wonder what the plan was going to be to keep a bunch of penned-up kids from going hog wild with boredom when Miss Chips stood up. She'd been sitting immobile near a side wall next to a traumatized-looking Coach Parker.

"Enough!" she yelled, and the kids quieted down. Not all the way—even Miss Chips's power couldn't subdue an entire auditorium—but when she stood up and glared, kids weakened. I wondered how she could still be so bitter over a failed fund-raiser. But Brillo pads? What was she thinking?

"Becky Binkey!" she yelled. And then she said the worst three words I could have possibly imagined. "Do the play!"

I swallowed loud enough that it could be heard over an auditorium full of groans.

"But we don't have the costumes or anything!" Becky said.

"Who cares, Binkey, just do it," said Miss Chips, sinking back into immobility.

I couldn't believe it. The thought of standing on that stage in front of my entire school was already hair-raising. But to be up there doing the lead role in a play, unprepared, with them all surly and savage and possibly believing I might have recently trapped a number of them in holes just to get ahead . . . It was the biggest nightmare I could imagine (and keep in mind I'd met a Giant Slug).

As I climbed onto the stage my knees could barely support my weight.

Ed's and Ted's faces had the malicious glee of someone about to watch the world's biggest piñata get pulverized by a Transformers robot. Marco still looked like he was trying to make me explode with his mind. Everyone else displayed a mix of expressions ideal for undermining confidence.

The Binkettes took their spots, and Becky took her place opposite me at center stage. And although my brain wasn't actually connected to my mouth at that moment, my mouth started saying the words I'd heard Marco say over and over in rehearsal. And I realized this was my big chance to win the kids' approval, or at least prevent myself from sliding all the way back to the bottom. To show everyone that I wasn't just some weird, mud-covered, eel-eating, graveyard-living oddball, but was, in fact, a completely normal kid.

And I was out there on the stage, doing my lines, getting things mostly right. And I started to feel pretty good. I started to believe I was going to make it. I started to think, *Hey, maybe from now on, everything is going to be okay* . . .

And then, as you may remember . . .

Weird things are drawn to me. It just always happens.

The worm hung in the air for a moment, resting in the silence of a room full of kids all sucking in their breath at once. Then it crashed to the stage floor, splattering worm mucus everywhere. Wood splintering. Kids screaming. Teachers yelling. And then it was gone.

If there'd been a frenzy before, it was multiplied by ten now. Kids were bouncing around like popcorn making as much noise with their mouths as they could muster. Becky wiped worm mucus from her eyes as some of the Binkettes—dedicated even during a crisis— surrounded her and started wiping her off with moisturizing facial wipes. I guess people like Becky *could* have gross things happen to them if they stood close enough to me.

Marco leapt onto the busted stage and leveled a finger at me like he was playing God in a play about a guy who was about to meet his judgment. "Underbelleeeeeeee!" he screamed unto me, unable to fix on a specific accusation.

And that was the end of my dabbling with popularity. All the damage that could possibly be done to my status was complete. As if to underline the point, the curtain along with its rods and poles, probably shaken loose by the giant worm, crashed down onto me and Marco. I used it as cover to crawl to stage left and flee the auditorium. And . . . *scene.*

I spent the next couple of hours hiding in my secret alcove behind the Brillo pads, listening to the sounds of the janitor's slop bucket moving up and down the hall and kids closing lockers and going home early.

As the distraction of popularity seeped away, it left my brain to get back to functioning regularly (such as it was). I started thinking about those emergency crown symbols I'd seen. *What could they be about? The rain?* I thought, hearing it continue to pound on a nearby window. The Moles must have survived heavy rain many times over who knows how many generations. So what could be causing emergency problems this time? Don't think I was forgetting about the giant worm that just exploded through the floor. But again, everything had been fine until now, so why would worms suddenly be an emergency? Was it just about the Moles having Up-stuff again? Was there another uproar about them being made to throw it all down the Big Hole—

And then it hit me. I figured out what the thing was that had changed. I needed to get down there right away. I needed to tell them what to do. But first, in order to do that, I needed something else.

I rushed out of the school and splashed toward home. When I got there, I veered left up the path to the white-picket-fence house as per usual, only I wasn't trying to pretend it was my home anymore, that fakery was done. Instead I ran around back and looked through a window.

Magda was inside, lying on a bed in a room

that showed the battle scars of a war being waged between the syrupy-sweet aesthetics of the homeowners and the funeral-chic defiance of their daughter.

I tapped on the window. She looked, then returned her eyes to the ceiling. I tapped again. Then some more. Then some more. When she looked back again her ping-pong eyes were squished flat. She came to the window.

"So, um, hey," I said, "y'know that plant holder? Um, well, it turns out it *is* a piece off one of the tombstones, from the grave of some guy who used to be the head of a giant plant holder company, and, uh, his relatives are coming by to visit, and it turns out whenever they come they always put a fresh plant in the plant holder, because it was like the plant holder guy's last wish to always have a fresh plant on his grave, since he liked plants and plant holders so much. Heh, crazy, eh?"

"Crazy. Yeah. Just like me, right?"

Magda's black mascara made it so that the more narrowed her eyes were, the more black they got. There was pretty much nothing but black.

"So, uh, can I get it back?"

She picked up the crown, held it through the window, and dropped it at my feet. Then pulled down the blind.

I picked it up and ran off. The King was back!

9

THE KING
IS DEPOSED

I found the Big Cavern in a state of total chaos. There was way more Up-stuff than last time, so much now that stuff was routinely being knocked into the Big Hole because there was nowhere else for it to go.

More alarmingly, there were a couple of Mega Worms lying next to holes that they'd recently erupted from. Everything was wet. The water was really backing up.

The cacophony of the Mole People was deafening. They quarreled over possessions and heaved things either at each other or randomly across the cavern. The lack of clarity in my last "decree" had again been catastrophic.

There was zero acknowledgment of my status as King. Any adulation was completely absent, as were smiles, pleasantries, or attention paid to the trajectory of thrown objects. If any Moles looked at me at all it was only to scowl. I'd been told that collective changes in Mole opinion happened quickly. I guess it was true.

"Well, look who decided to show up!" the squeakiest of Mole voices called out from atop the royal platform. "Your no-good, goof-off, thinks-he's-better-than-us King has finally decided to grace us with his presence!"

Croogy had pulled his comfortable-looking chair right up next to the throne and was using the throne as a footrest.

"King!" yelled Oog, who was wearing a megaphone as a hat and fighting with another Mole over a trench coat.

Oog picked me up and plowed through the Mole throng, and I scrambled to the top of the ramp. I screamed to everyone that I

had an important message, but I could barely hear myself over the noise. I grabbed Oog's megaphone hat and pressed the button that set off the super-loud siren. All the Moles paused and looked my way.

"Listen, I'm sorry I didn't come sooner!" I called out. "I realize I failed you, but—"

"He failed us!" yelled Croogy. "Just like I warned you! You can't trust a human!"

Everybody booed. It was becoming a habit

for me to be the focus of crowd anger.

"Wait! I'm here to help you!" I yelled. "The Mega Worms are coming up from below! If they keep coming they're going to destroy the Mole kingdom and maybe even the Up-world too!"

"Aha, so he only showed up because he's worried about his precious human world!" yelled Croogy.

"Are worms really coming all the way to the Up-world?" said Ploogoo, who had just clawed his way onto the platform. "Why is this happening?"

"Remember how I told you little worms come to the surface when there's too much water in the ground?" I said. "Well, picture that but on a much, much larger—"

At that moment there was a huge noise, and a giant worm exploded from the floor. And when I say giant, I mean like the size of a pickup truck. It flopped about all soggy and gross.

"We don't have to picture it!" said a slimy voice. We all turned to see the Slug Ambassador sliming toward us. "The Slug level is getting overrun with Mega Worms right now! We've done our part, Croogy! The Slug King now demands you keep your end of the, y'know . . ."

Croogy looked anxious for a moment, then pointed at the Slug: "It's the Slugs that are causing the worms to rise! They're attacking!"

"It's not the Slugs!" I yelled. "I know what's causing the water to back up, and I know how to fix it! The other night I was taking a bath and all the grubs that were on me went down the drain and clogged it! I had to get a plunger and a long-handled screwdriver to—"

"He can't even wash himself without causing problems!" yelled Croogy.

"Just listen to me, and if after that you want to depose me as your King—"

"Depose him!" yelled Croogy. "*Depose the human!*" Then he stood and lifted his arms over the crowd. "I propose a new era of Mole supremacy! First we'll squash the loathsome Slugs and the rest of the lower denizens, then we'll rise up and vanquish the humans and take our rightful place as rulers of the Upworld!"

They took a moment to get on board, but the throng was already revved up, and the idea of having all the problems fixed sounded good. Once part of a crowd gets started cheering, it's easy for the rest of the crowd to join in.

"And to lead you in this righteous journey, you need a new King!" yelled Croogy.

He snatched the crown, then held it over my head—the Moles rumbled lowly. Then he held it over his own head—and the rumble thundered through the cavern. With that, he lowered the crown onto himself.

Then he kicked the old painful throne off the royal platform.

"But you're the one who made me be King!" I said.

"Do you think I'd ever really let a human be King of the Mole People?" he said, pushing his comfortable chair into the throne's former place. "I knew I'd never win the Crown Rumble after Zog. With all the disgusting human love, even Oog might've beat me after bringing down that stupid royal shovel! So I thought, if they're so nuts for humans, why not find some pitiful one to give the crown to so they could see how terrible humans really are!

"I didn't expect I'd get lucky enough to find one as pathetic and easily manipulated as you! I could barely stomach listening to you whine to your tombstone buddies about how unpopular you are. The only thing I can't believe is how long it took for the Moles to start detesting you and all your human junk! Well, at least it's finally sunk in!"

This was like one of those cliché movie scenes where the bad guy explains what his plan was for no real reason. Nobody ever did that in real life. But Moles never watched movies, so I guess it didn't seem cliché to Croogy.

He then turned and gave his first order to

his subjects. "Throw all this human garbage down the Big Hole!" And all the Moles started angrily obeying.

"No! You're going to make the situation worse!" I yelled.

"Yes, a clog. Getting worse and worse. Giving me the idea about the worms was the only useful thing you ever did."

"So I take it you're not keeping your end of the bargain with the Slugs?" said the ambassador.

"Throw the Slug Ambassador down the hole!" commanded Croogy.

The Moles grabbed the ambassador and began shoving his globulous mass toward the hole.

"Now, wait a minute," said Ploogoo. "Maybe we're being a bit rash—"

"The Slugs will get you for this!" yelled the ambassador. "We'll rise up and destroy the Moles! All of yooooooouuuu . . ." And with that last statement, down the hole he went, a huge gush of air escaping his mouth as he fell.

"Not if we destroy you first!" yelled Croogy. "Boogo! Take a group of our best diggers and start digging under the creek!"

"Boog," said Boogo in a low voice, and you could tell from his tone that he wasn't a fan of this idea.

"But that much water could cause the worms to destroy *everything*!" I said.

"Why is he still talking?" said Croogy.

"Royal Guard, *seize him!*"

"King run!!" yelled Oog.

"Yes, Your Majesty. I suggest you flee," said Ploogoo.

"Royal Guard, you are hereby stripped of your status!" said Croogy. "Seize them too!"

Frenzied Moles fell upon Oog, Boogo, and Ploogoo, and they all started grappling. Oog turned toward me and yelled, "TGIF!"

It was Thursday, but I knew what he was really saying was to get the heck out of there. The Moles were in a mob state, bellowing and tossing everything into the Big Hole. I saw a group of Moles struggling with the royal statue of me. The grimace of pain on the statue's face looked extra appropriate as it toppled into the darkness.

I turned and smashed my head on a stalactite. Stars obliterated my vision as I stumbled into the tunnel and ran for home.

10

LOWEST
POINT EVER
(FIGURATIVELY)

I woke up in my bed with a giant goose egg on my head. I'd been lying there for about a day with a splitting headache, feeling sorry for myself. Not only was I back to having no popularity, but now, for the first time, I was despised both above the surface and below it. I had attained a level of unpopularity no creature on planet Earth had ever before experienced.

I've heard that some people feel a sense of ease at being at the lowest point you can go, taking comfort in the notion that at least it can't get any worse. I took no such comfort. I was friendless. And I'd possibly caused the end of the world as we know it. I was inconsolable.

"Howdy, sport. Feeling any better?" said my dad, entering the room carrying a tray. *Great*, I thought, *here comes the eel train.*

EEL SOUP

EEL MAC 'N' CHEESE

EEL ICE CREAM

"I know you're feeling down, so I fixed you some comfort food. Comfort food always makes you feel better."

I took a slurp of the soup. I'm not sure if

it was my despair, or if I was just getting used to it, but I was growing more and more fond of my dad's creations. I did feel comforted.

"You like it?" asked Dad.

I told him it was delicious. Which I guess was the encouragement he needed to reveal his "big news." He said he'd finally come up with the answer to our "troubled finances." He moved to the center of the room as if he was giving a presentation.

"I'm going to put out a book of recipes for eel!"

I slurped. And told him the idea was wonderful. But that I couldn't help but wonder if he might do better making recipes for food people would more regularly consider eating.

"Well, that's the thing," he said. "There are already thousands of cookbooks for more traditional food. But nobody's doing eels! If you do the same thing as everybody else, it's impossible to stand out. If you want to get somewhere, it's better to be different. Maybe. Or maybe that's not right, either. Maybe the best thing is to not even think about it. Just let the world rush over you, and pluck out little pieces of it that you like the look of, and use them to build a little version of yourself inside you that keeps you being the real, true version of you. Do you know what I mean, son?"

I had no idea what he was talking about. But he seemed very enthusiastic about this eel book, and he was my dad, and I wanted him to be happy.

He smiled and winked at me. Then tasted the soup. "Needs something. More basil!" And he bounced merrily from the room.

I was raising a forkful of eel mac 'n' cheese when I noticed something on my window. It was a crown, drawn in mud. I couldn't believe it. What could they possibly want from me now?

Then the window opened and in climbed Magda. I pretended to be asleep.

"I can tell you're awake, Underbelly," she said. "You're holding a forkful of mac 'n' cheese."

When I kept my eyes closed she lobbed my

exploded sneaker at me and it hit me on the goose egg. "Ow!" I said.

"I knew that thing wasn't a plant holder!" she said, jumping onto my bed. Her knowing smile was back and her eyes were ping-pongs again. "I can't believe you were King of the Mole People and didn't want the job! I'd *love* that job!"

"Of course *you'd* want a job like that," I said. "If such a thing existed. Which it doesn't. Mole People, what a crazy thing to—"

"Oh, please, enough with the denial. You're shot socially anyways." And she opened the window wider to accommodate Oog's huge head.

"There you are, King!" he said. "Dark Eyes help us find you. This first time in history Mole ever climb tree!"

It seems my Royal Guard had been leaving mud trails all over the block looking for me before finally running into Magda. Apparently with such short-range vision they never knew about second floors.

"Ooo, now *this* kingly room!" said Oog, leaping to the bed and then gasping as he looked around. "Oog see so many things he hear King talk about to tombstones! Old Hot Wheels you love when small! Magician hat from time King try to be magician! Karate outfit from time King sign up for karate after get beat up for try to be magician! Ooo! This picture of King's dad? He not as creepy looking as King say."

He held up a comic book featuring a zombie, making me feel bad for all the times I'd compared my father unfavorably to ghouls. "No," I said, pointing at a picture. "That's him there, with me."

"Ah, from time he take you fun park! And you throw up on spinny ride! And then again at squirt-gun game. And then again in car on ride home—"

"This Oog guy really cares about you for some reason," said Magda. "Guess you haven't stabbed him in the back yet."

"Sorry about that," I said. "I was still clinging to some hope of normal. Now I've got Mole People in my bedroom."

"I'm sorry too, for not telling you I lived in the Precious Moments house," said Magda.

Then the scene got a little awkward, until Oog broke the silence by slurping a spoonful of the soup off my tray. "Needs something," he said. "More grubs!"

"Careful, Master Digger!" said Ploogoo, who had now appeared in the window. His arms were tightly wrapped about Boogo's neck as Boogo climbed from the tree to the ledge. "Moles aren't supposed to be this high aboveground."

I was happy to see the Guard had all made it out of the Big Cavern. Croogy had been in the process of removing their Os and demoting them down to Og, Bog, and Plog, when he spotted the female Mole with the big horn and the pet real mole and started yelling "No pet moles!", giving the Royal Guard an opportunity to escape through some back tunnels they'd been using to access the surface. On top of all his other shortcomings, Croogy also hated cute pets.

"What King doing lying in bed?" asked Oog.

"Didn't you hear? I was never your King. Croogy just used me because I'm pathetic."

Magda slipped in her quick agreement, and I told them what Croogy had told me about using me to help him take over, and how bad his breath was up close. Ploogoo agreed about the breath, but said he and the rest of the Royal Guard rejected Croogy's takeover, and that as far as they were concerned I was still King.

"But I was a terrible King," I said. "All I did was complain about the painful throne and the dirty water."

"That may be true," said Ploogoo. "But we can't let Croogy start a war just so he can win the crown from you," said Ploogoo.

"We be crummy Royal Guard if we let that happen," said Oog. "And crummy friends."

"You really still want me as your King?"

"Former King Zog had a dream of harmonizing the Moles and the humans," said Ploogoo. "As you could see, the Moles were in favor of this dream. You won the Crown Rumble. You represented the Mole People's wishes."

"Plus King hilarious!" said Oog. "The way King smash head on way out of overthrow. King always have such great timing!"

"Kinnnnng," said Boogo, putting a huge hand on my shoulder.

"You're so clueless, Underbelly. You don't even know when people like you," said Magda.

"Okay, I get it, Magda, the Moles like me."

"I think Dark Eyes saying *she* like King!" said Oog, smiling. "Oog knew it! King her boyfriend!"

"He's not my boyfriend!" yelled Magda.

"You protest too—"

At that moment there came a terrible sound from the backyard, and we looked out my window to see this:

KER-PASSSH

SIZE OF MINI SCHOOL BUS

"Why are they still coming up?" I asked in alarm. "Don't tell me Croogy is still getting Moles to dig under the creek??"

"Boooooog!" said Boogo.

"Boogo says even though he refuse, Croogy send other Moles to dig," said Oog. "But he say it not possible Moles dig through to creek yet."

"It must still be backed up down there from all the rain," I said. "If they dig through to the creek it'll release a tidal wave!"

"This must be Croogy's plan to defeat the Slugs," said Ploogoo. "He reneged on some sort of deal with them. Now they're preparing to retaliate."

"Much angry belching coming from below," said Oog.

It seemed like that much water could send up enough Worms to destroy the Slug level, but would the Worms stop there? If they were already starting to pop up in the Up-world, I shuddered to think of what would happen if the whole creek got unleashed.

"And look at the size of them!" said Magda. "They're huge!"

"That not huge Worm," said Oog. "That baby. Adults twenty times bigger."

"And there are hundreds of them," said Ploogoo meekly.

The "baby" Mega Worm sloshed around in the puddle, knocking over tombstones, filling us with the dread of what hundreds of adult worms might do.

"Croogy always dreamed of crushing the human scum into the dirt (his words)," said Ploogoo. "The Worms will rip everything to shreds. Then he'll lead the Moles to take over the remains."

But his plan only worked if the water didn't drain away, and the only reason it wasn't draining was because the Big Hole was clogged with Up-stuff. It was like a bathtub drain filled with grubs. You needed to get right down in there to the clog and unblock it.

"We need unclog clog!" said Oog.

"But to get to the clog you'd have to travel

past the Mole People level, and then get past the Slug level, and then pass through the realms of the Stone Goons and Mushroom Folk," said Ploogoo. "That would take negotiation only a King could handle."

"Right. Wait, you mean *me?*" I said. "No, no, no, no! I may have been enough of a sucker to let you crush my neck with a fifty-pound crown, but that sounds like actual bravery stuff. I'm not brave, I'm a coward! You got the wrong Up-worlder!"

"Oh brother." Magda rolled her eyes. "The last thing I feel like doing is giving you a pep talk, Underbelly. Sheesh, yes, you're pretty pathetic, but you *are* brave. You crack jokes in front of Miss Chips. You told Becky Binkey you had a crush on her in front of all the Binkettes. You stood on a stage in front of a whole school of kids who can't stand you or the way you look or the way you smell—"

"I thought this was a pep talk," I said.

"You went down into a grave hole and hung out with a society of underground Mole

People. Like it or not, you're brave."

I didn't know if I agreed with Magda. I felt like she might be mixing up boldness and desperation. A drowning rat splashing madly in the water isn't exactly brave.

But maybe being at rock bottom gave me some strength after all. Or maybe it felt good to be wanted by a group. Or maybe it was the sound of tombstones being crushed by the giant "baby" Mega Worm slithering around in the backyard. I'd already demonstrated that I was willing to go to some pretty great lengths to satisfy any groups I passingly believed I was a part of. So if the Mole People were my true, actual group, what was a little self-destructive journey to the center of the earth?

I threw off the covers, stood up, and raised a clenched fist. "All right! Let's do it! Let's unclog that clog! Let's save the world! Weirdness, you are always drawn to me! You never leave me alone! Well, this time, weirdness . . . *I'm coming for you!*"

INSPIRATIONAL STANCE

FORGOT WAS WEARING RUBBER DUCKY UNDERWEAR

11

LOWEST POINT EVER (LITERALLY)

Ploogoo was apprehensive. "It might be pretty tricky for *all* of us to sneak through so many territories . . ."

I told him he was right as I quickly pulled on shorts. I had assignments for everyone. I turned to Master Digger Boogo, who had become enamored with my soccer headband, and said I needed him to go fill in what the other Moles were digging away and try to hold back the water as long as possible. He said "Boog" heartily and flexed his digging muscles. Then I told Magda I needed her to go get a box.

"What?" she said, not heartily at all. "The

fate of everything we know is at stake and you want me to be a courier? I want to do the important stuff!"

"All the missions are equally important," I said, filling my backpack for the journey. "I need you to get the big gray box from the science portable. I will hear no further argument, this is my royal decree!"

"Oh, *now* you're going to start acting like a king?" she said.

I told Ploogoo he needed to go with Magda and help her sneak the box down into the Mole Kingdom to the top of the Big Hole and then wait there for my signal. Then I turned to Oog.

"Oog, buddy, I need you to accompany me, your King and friend, on the most important mission. I need you to help guide me through those secret back tunnels on an intrepid journey deep into the heart of the earth. Are you ready?"

"We have saying in Mole culture," said Oog. "It roughly translate as, 'Make sure grub not rock before you eat.' It not make sense here, but Oog ready."

"We can stay in touch using these," I said, pulling out some old walkie-talkies and handing one to Magda. "Okay, I think we're ready to do this!"

"Seriously, 'decree'?" snorted Magda.

"That's right, decree. I decree something. Decree. Mole team ready?" I said, ignoring Magda's eye roll and pulling my backpack over my shoulder.

KINGLY AURA

BACKPACK FULL OF "ESSENTIALS"

HOLDING UP "RABBIT EARS" BEHIND KING IS PUNISHABLE OFFENSE (OR SHOULD BE)

"Let's go!" I yelled.

And we split up and headed off.

Oog and I ran into the backyard, past the Mega Worm, and dropped into the open grave hole. We headed in the opposite direction from the Big Cavern so we didn't run into any Moles. Oog said the Slug level was packed with Slugs, so we needed to go to the outer reaches of it to have any chance of getting through without being seen.

Eventually we ran out of Mole tunnel, and Oog said this was where we'd head downward. He dug for a while until his hole opened into a tunnel below: the Slug level.

It was covered in slime and smelled like burps. Unlike the Mole tunnels, the Slug tunnels seemed to shoot in every direction, and there were fields of fluorescent green algae that I figured were the Slug version of farms. But there weren't any Slugs tending them. All the Slugs we saw were marching soldiers.

They were clearly immersed in preparations

SLUG SOLDIERS

ASSUMED BECAUSE OF SPEARS

MARCHING
(ASSUMED, ACTUALLY REGULAR SLOW SLUG SPEED)

for hostilities, and this state of agitation caused them to belch incessantly, so they were easy to detect. Whenever we heard some coming, Oog would dig us into a wall and cover us with slime dirt while they slowly oozed past. A couple of them stopped right in front of us for a while, and I heard them making some comments about Croogy being a no-good backstabber and about how they could totally crush a plate of algae right about now.

What was harder to avoid were the Worms. We'd seen some on the Mole level, but the Slug level was seeping with water, and a Worm—twice as big as the ones I'd seen before (but still a "youngster," according to Oog)—exploded from the earth in front of us and almost took our heads off. We jumped out of the way just in time.

"At least it's a lot easier moving around down here without that crown on," I said to Oog.

"Oog never realize King so short," said Oog.

Once we were able to make our way into a quiet side tunnel, Oog started digging downward again until he hit rock. He dug all around it and revealed straight edges on the sides, like a really large brick. Then he pried one end up and we squeezed under it and dropped into the level of the Stone Goons.

The Stone Goon tunnels were immediately distinguishable from the other levels on account of they were lined with heavy blocks of stone. A bit of water trickled between the cracks, but for the most part the blocks seemed to be keeping the water out.

"What are Stone Goons like, anyway?" I asked.

"Oh, they big, heavy, and hard," said Oog.

"You just described a stone," I said.

"Yeah. They made of stone," said Oog.

We moved slowly and kept a sharp ear. The walls being lined with stone meant that Oog wasn't going to be able to dig any quick holes for us to hide in. We followed the stone-lined tunnel until it opened out into a room that had no other exits.

"Dead end," I said.

"Not dead end," said Oog. "We surrounded by Goons."

And then I realized that lots of the areas I thought were walls were actually beings who were made of stone.

"Who dares disturb the Stone Goons?" said one of the walls or beings. Their voices were deep and sounded like a bucket of gravel being poured out.

CAN YOU SPOT THE DIFFERENCE?

"This King Doug, King of the Mole People!" proclaimed Oog.

"Well, I'm *sort* of King," I mumbled. "It's a bit complicated—"

"King, we already go through this!" said Oog. "You King! We love you! Say it big and proud!"

"Okay, all right," I said, and turned back to the Stones. "Um, is there, like, a Stone leader I could talk to?"

"We have no leader. The Stone Goons are all equals."

"Oh," I said. "Like a bunch of worker ants!"

There was a long pause. "What are you doing here?" said one.

I told the "People of the Stone" (how I addressed them in an effort to sound distinguished but immediately regretted as corny) that we meant no disrespect but only required safe passage through their fair kingdom. They grumbled at the word "kingdom," and I thought it was going to be because they had no king, but it turned out it was because they thought calling this a "fair kingdom" was making light of the fact that they lived in an area of cold, dark muck buried so deep in the ground that no one knows it exists.

"It's nice what you've done with it," I offered.

"You think it's easy down here?" said a Goon. "It's not. When you're made of stone, even walking around is a monumental task. And everything's made of big stone blocks. You have to carry stones nonstop. Our backs are shot."

"Do you know about lifting with your legs?" I said.

"Yes, of course we know about lifting with our legs! What, you think you're just going to waltz in here and solve all our lifting problems with one little suggestion? We've been lifting things for centuries!"

"All right, sorry. I didn't mean anything. I understand your pain."

"You?" scoffed a different Goon. "What do you know about lifting pain?"

"Well, actually," I said, "I spent some time as the water boy on a soccer team. I had to carry loads and loads of water."

The Stone Goons started mumbling. Their expressions never changed—they were incapable of changing—so it was hard to tell what they were thinking. But it became apparent my water boy story had struck a positive chord.

"Water is a lot heavier than it looks," said a Goon.

"Tell me about it!" I said, and then pressed ahead while I had the advantage. I told them we needed passage because the Slug People were going to attack the Mole People, and the Mole People were going to attack both the Slug People and the humans using Mega Worms. And we needed to get to the bottom of the Big Hole and remove the giant clog, or everybody was going to be in terrible danger, including them!

"We're made of rock," said a Goon. "We don't really have much to worry about."

Another pause.

"But the idea of beings from different levels helping each other is a welcome change," said another. "You may pass."

I'd done it! I'd successfully negotiated our way through the Stone Goon area. The Goons seemed like reasonable creatures who had a hard lot in life stuck down so deep. So, in the spirit of harmony between our different levels,

I reached into my backpack and pulled out a small ray of Up-world sunshine to brighten their dismal lives.

"Please accept this royal gift as a token of our appreciation. If I see you again, I'll get the container back, but if not, just keep it."

"What is this?"

"It's eel mac 'n' cheese. Y'know, for eating. Here, try a bite."

I pushed a forkful into the Goon's mouth. Instantly the Goon started violently choking. How was I to know they ingested rock for sustenance and had never eaten food before? I tried slapping the choking Goon on the back but hurt my hand on the hard slab of its torso.

A couple of the other Goons pulled some stones apart for us to pass through. I was happy to hear the gravel-pail sounds of his choking subsiding before the stones slammed shut behind us with a foreboding BOOM!

We were now in the realm of the Mushroom Folk.

The tunnels on the Mushroom Folk level looked more organic, like they were grown instead of dug. And I was sorry for calling the Slug People tunnels "slimy," because the Mushroom Folk tunnels put a whole new spin on slime. They were gooey and slippery and sopping wet. And of course, they reeked of mushrooms.

The Stone Goon interaction had worked out well enough that I was feeling pretty confident in my diplomacy skills. And I was actually looking forward to meeting this next group of beings, as "folk" made them sound like good-natured country types.

"They not that way at all," said Oog. "They super grumpy."

"No problem," I said. "I can handle a little grumpy."

"Who dares call the Mushroom Folk grumpy?" boomed a deep, gooey voice.

And suddenly we realized we'd been walking through a forest of mushrooms with faces. Angry, bitter faces. They ranged in size from upright polar bears all the way down to as tiny as you could see. One in particular was extra huge and his "top" was pointy and flecked with gold. I took him to be their king and addressed him directly.

"It is I! Doug Underbelly, King of the Mole People!"

The Mushroom Folk had a very distinct response to this . . .

"Don't yell about being King around Mushroom Folk!" said Oog. "They threatened by other royalty!"

"Why the heck didn't you tell me that?" I cried.

"We'll strip the skin from your bones and grow ourselves from the eye sockets in your skulls!" bellowed the Mushroom King.

"And get under your fingernails and cause them to turn black and fall off!" said a surprisingly angry tiny mushroom.

Well, my diplomacy had gone off the rails

fast. I pleaded with them to hold off on their assaults to our eye sockets and fingernails and told them we were merely trying to get to the bottom of the Big Hole so we could prevent Mega Worms yadda yadda yadda, and that in the spirit of different species helping each other for a change, might we please have safe passage through their . . . kingdom?

"The Mushroom kingdom is the greatest kingdom ever known! We do not permit the contamination of foreign bodies!" yelled the angry king.

"I understand that life down here must not be easy for you," I offered.

"The life of a Mushroom is fantastic! Mushrooms are the most superior beings of all! We turn rot and decay into glorious nutrients! You'd all be nothing without us!"

"We spit on the rest of you! *P-tui!*" yelled the tiny one.

Finding common ground had worked well with the Stone Goons, so I thought I'd try the same tactic with the Mushrooms. I told them I agreed that things that grew from the ground were the most glorious things of all, and that I knew what it was like standing in one spot for long periods of time since I'd spent some time in the school play playing a shrub.

The Mushroom Folk started mumbling. Unlike the Stone Goons, their expressions were comically exaggerated, so I could tell immediately if my tactic had worked. Of course their angry shouts would have tipped me off regardless.

"Infidel!"

"You dare mock us?"

"You're comparing us to shrubs??"

"No!" I scrambled. "I don't think so! I like mushrooms! They're delicious!"

"Gasp! *WHAT??*" the Mushroom King boomed.

"Wait, I was lying!" I scrambled more. "I just said that because I thought that's what you'd want to hear! I can't stand the taste of mushrooms! If I accidentally get one in my mouth I hock it out just as fast as I can!"

"We better wrap this up," said Oog.

"I'd love to. Any ideas?"

"Yeah. We walk round them," said Oog. "They not able to move."

"Dude, you really need to be more forth-coming with information!"

The Mushroom Folk continued their hair-raising barrage of threats as we stepped past them, stuff about feasting on our flesh, laying spores in our brains, and blackening the soles of our feet.

"Watch it!" screeched the tiny one.

"You almost stepped on my son!" yelled their king.

They all leaned toward us, yelling, "Attack! Attack!" and spitting and vibrating with fury. But their stalks held them fast to the ground. We stepped gingerly around them, careful not to step on any of the little ones.

"Royal gift from the Mole King!" I called when we'd reached the far side, and tossed a container back at them.

SPLOOSH!

MELTED EEL ICE CREAM

We hurried off down the tunnel to their echoing descriptions of what mushroom-y atrocities they would inflict if we were inclined to lie still beside them for an extended period of time.

"That didn't go well at all," I said.

"Diplomacy not work on the super grumpy," said Oog.

As we proceeded, the tunnels turned from gooey back to muddy and continued sloping downward, getting more and more soggy. We started seeing car-size worms wriggling around in puddles, and then some bus-size worms. Then we saw one the size of a subway car. I hoped this was the biggest one we'd come across as I was out of transportation-vehicle comparisons.

I decided I'd better check on Magda's progress.

"Eagle to Squirrel. Come in, Squirrel," I said into the walkie-talkie.

"Who's Squirrel?" came Magda's staticky reply.

"You're Squirrel. I came up with code names."

"You can't just come up with code names without telling me. How am I supposed to know who I'm talking to?"

"Who else could you be talking to? These are only two-way walkie-talkies!"

"Well, then why would we need code names?"

"Because we're on a mission!" I said.

"And why would you be 'Eagle'? Eagles fly in the air. You're deep under the ground."

"Well, 'mole' is a little on the nose, don't you think?"

"If anything *I* should be Eagle and *you* should be Squirrel," Magda said.

"I already picked the names!"

"But Squirrel makes no sense!" she yelled.

"*You* make no sense!" I yelled back.

"You two so in love," said Oog. "You should do kissing."

"We're not in love!" "Nobody's kissing!" "In your dreams!" we both yelled at once.

"King, shhh!" said Oog, pointing. "Look!"

We'd reached the clog.

12

THE CLOG

The Big Hole was a lot thinner this far down, and the pile of stuff it was clogged with was enough to choke a department store. I saw the playground slide, that section of white picket fence, my royal statue with the pained face. Water trickled down the walls onto the clog and was soaking into the earth around it.

We also noticed a couple of Slug guards. We crouched down quickly behind a bunch of the clog debris before realizing they were both asleep.

"I wonder what they're guarding?" I whispered.

"Look at pile of stuff!" whispered Oog.

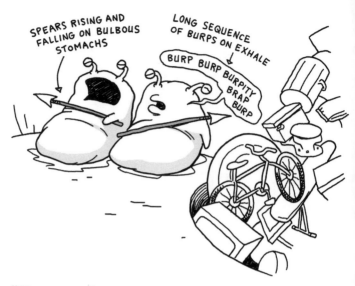

"How two of us going to unclog such big clog?"

"With science, my good Mole, with science," and I turned to my walkie-talkie. "Are you there, Squirrel?"

"Eagle here," said Magda.

"I already told you, *I'm* Eagle!" I whisper-yelled.

"Why are you in charge of names?"

"Because I'm King and these are my walkie-talkies!"

I decreed that she stop fighting me about the names and tell me if they'd got the box from the science portable. She gave me another hard time about using the word "decree" and then told me she and Ploogoo had the box and were waiting at the top of the Big Hole, and did I want her to drop it? I told her yes.

"Oh, but try to drop it on the left side of the hole," I said. "There are some Slugs on the—"

"Too late, I already dropped it," said Magda.

WHAP! The box landed right on the Slugs' heads, then bounced off and disappeared into a small pit we hadn't noticed. The Slug guards belched loudly and awoke.

"Who goes there?!" demanded the first Slug.

"'Who goes there?' What kind of talk is that?" said the second Slug.

"I dunno. Feels like what guards say," said the first.

I crouched down and backed into a bike horn. HONK!

"Who goes there?!" demanded the second Slug.

"Oh, so it's okay if *you* say it??" said the first Slug.

"Well, now that you said it, you put it in my head," said the second.

"So if I say 'peanut,' you're just gonna say 'peanut'?" said the first.

"We may have got lucky," I whispered to Oog.

I backed into the horn again. HONK!

They leveled their spears at us and shoved us into the pit. It was small and lined with stones that looked like they might have been swiped from the Stone Goon area, and we realized it was a makeshift prison. Mostly because it had a prisoner.

Oog recognized our fellow captive immediately.

"King Zooooooooooooooooog!" he shouted.

"Oog!" said the prisoner.

"The former King?" I stammered.

"It's so great to see you!" said the King, embracing Oog. "And who is *this*?" he asked, turning toward me like I was the most interesting person in the world. "A human! An actual human! Down here under the ground!"

FORMER KING

DEBONAIR FOR A MOLE

SURPRISINGLY GOOD SPIRITS FOR A KIDNAPPED PERSON

"Nice to meet you, King Zoooooooo—"

"Please, I never went in for all those Os even when I had a crown on my head," he said, vigorously shaking my hand. "Just call me Zog. I'm so glad you're here! As if I wasn't intrigued enough by your human stuff already, being stuck for weeks beside this growing pile of wonders has been unbearable! I've been dying to know—what's that thing with two circles on it?"

"It's a bike," I said.

"Wait! I recognize that voice!" said Zog, turning toward me with his tiny eyes lit up. "You're the human from the graveyard! The one Oog and I spent hours listening in on while you filled in holes and talked about the hilarious trials of your fascinating Up-life! I was captivated! Before I heard you, I thought the same thing all Moles thought, that humans were destructive and dangerous. But you were so goofy and funny! I don't know how many times you stepped on that shovel and I heard it flip up and smack you in the head!"

"He the funniest guy ever!" said Oog.

"You're the reason we started loving humans, right, Oog?" said Zog, clapping his huge hands on my shoulders and lifting me up off the ground. "It is such a pleasure! Oh, so many questions! What's a 'goalpost'? What's a 'noogie'? What's 'eel pad thai'?"

Oog intervened and explained that there was a reason I was there that was somewhat time-sensitive. He told Zog that when he disappeared the Moles assumed he was dead, and that Croogy brought me down from the Up-world for the Crown Rumble and I won. Zog thought this was fantastic, and that in his wild imaginings of Mole/human unity he never dreamed it would move so fast. Then Oog told him how Croogy set me up to be despised and deposed and how he started a war with the Slugs just to win the Crown Rumble. Zog thought this wasn't as fantastic.

"It's so surprising that Croogy betrayed us all like this," said Zog.

"Surprising? Really?" I said. "I know this might seem like hindsight, but isn't Croogy pretty obviously crummy? He even hates cute little mole pets."

"That wasn't always the case," said Zog. "He had a mole pet himself when he was just a little Mole. It ran up to the surface and Croogy went after it. It jumped on a truck and the truck sped away. Croogy never saw it again."

"So all this bitterness and dislike of humans comes from losing his pet mole?"

"Hmm, that might be going a little far . . ." said Zog before his attention drifted onto the pile of stuff. "So how does a 'bike' work, King Doug?"

"The circles are wheels, and you ride it by—King? *You're* the King."

Zog shuffled his feet against the stones. "Well, to be honest, I was kind of thinking about giving up being King. Which I told Croogy. He wanted to be my successor, but he knew the Moles would never accept him. So he told the Slugs I was planning on crushing the Slug scum into the dirt (his words) and then made a deal with them: if they helped him become Mole King, he'd let them have the Mole level when he and the Moles took over the Up-world. All the Slugs had to do was 'get rid of' me. So I've been stuck down here in this pit ever since."

"Zog must be big angry at Croogy!" said Oog.

"I guess." Zog shrugged. "But I never wanted to be King anyway!"

"Well, I never wanted to be King either!" I said. "Since you're alive, you get to go back to being King!"

"Now Oog not know who to call King," said Oog.

"Never mind, we have more pressing issues at hand," I said. "Croogy's ordered Moles to dig under the creek to release the water down this hole!"

"Won't that drive up all the Mega Worms, Your Majesty?" said Zog.

"Stop that! Yes, but we can unclog the drain," I said, opening the box and pulling out the rockets that were inside, "by using these!"

Oog and Zog stared at the magical items in wonder.

"Behold the awe-inspiring power of science!" I said, lighting the fuses on all the rockets and pointing them at the mountain of debris. "Stand back!" I yelled.

And the rockets fired.

BOOM! BOOM! BOOM!

"Whooooa . . . !" said Zog, completely enthralled. "They're beauuuuutiful . . . !"

"They had no effect at all!" I cried.

"Halt!" yelled the first Slug.

"'Halt'?" said the second Slug. "They're already in a hole."

"Why are you ragging on me, man?" said the first.

"I'm sorry. I'm tired," said the second.

"These long guard hours are wrecking me."

"Hey you, guards!" I yelled from the pit. "There's going to be more than long hours wrecking you if you don't let us out of here and help us unclog this hole!"

"Pipe down in there!" yelled the Slugs.

"I demand you bring the Slug King here at once!" I yelled.

The Slug guards laughed, and Oog and Zog chuckled too.

"Why is that funny?" I said.

"Slug King so huge, he can't move," said Oog.

"It takes a really big Slug to win the Great Slugging," said Zog.

"The Slug King doesn't speak to prisoners of war!" boomed a new voice, and we saw the Slug Ambassador oozing onto the scene. He slithered up next to the guards and stared down into the pit. "Looks like we got enough Kings around here, anyway."

"Listen, Slug Ambassador, we're all in serious danger!" I called.

"Oh, and you're here to save us?" said the ambassador. "Typical upper-level arrogance! We Slug People have had enough of being treated like bags of slime! We're ready to unleash fury!"

The water running down the sides of the hole was steadily increasing.

The Mole diggers must have been getting close to breaking through to the creek.

"This is your last chance, Zog!" yelled the ambassador. "Tell us where the secret tunnels are that lead to the Mole level and we'll spare your life!"

"Wait, Slug Ambassador!" I said. "I know

you don't want to do this. I know you Slugs are good and decent people."

"We're not good! We're bad! We're tough and mean!"

"When Croogy told you to get rid of King Zog, he probably meant for you to kill him. But you didn't," I said. "And you're only angry at the Moles because you thought Zog wanted to attack you. But that was just a lie Croogy told you to trick you into helping him!"

"He said you called us scum!" said the Slug Ambassador petulantly.

"King Zog never said that!" I said. "In fact, King Zog has a dream of the beings of all levels living together in harmony!"

"That's ridiculous," said the ambassador. "*All* the beings?"

"Well, probably not the Mushroom Folk, but—"

"Now you're just spewing desperate nonsense! For all we know you've been in on this with Croogy the whole time! We're not falling for any more backstabs!" He belched with furious anger. "The attack will go ahead as planned!"

Suddenly Magda's voice buzzed over the walkie-talkie. "Eagle to Squirrel! Come in, Squirrel!"

"*I'm* Eagle! I already told you, *I'm* Eagle!" I yelled.

"Heh heh, you two. Do the kissing already," said Oog.

"Nobody is kissing!" I yelled.

"Yes, nobody is kissing, or doing anything else for that matter," came a squeaky Mole voice over the speaker. It was Croogy. He'd discovered Magda and Ploogoo.

I could hear some other Moles talking to Ploogoo. "Hi, Ploogoo." "How's it going?" And then Croogy angrily yelling, "Quit saying hi to him! He's an enemy of the Moles! *Seize them!*"

There was a commotion and a squeal. I couldn't tell if it was from Magda or Ploogoo.

"Stay back, Croogy!" I yelled into the walkie-talkie.

"How do you know my name, human?" said Croogy. "And why do you talk without moving your lips?"

Oog saw the look of confusion on my face. "Croogy not know what is walkie-talk box," he whispered. "He think your voice is voice of Dark Eyes."

"Who are you, human?" we heard Croogy demand.

I spoke into the walkie-talkie, raising my voice slightly to try to sound more girlish in case that helped with the illusion. "My name is Squirrel," I said.

We could hear Croogy snort. "Even for a human that's a stupid name."

"I think the name is perfect for me," I said. "And my mouth doesn't move when I talk because I was probably dropped on my head as a baby. Also please excuse my weird, dark eyes. I put on too much makeup as a way to rebel against my parents."

Through the speaker we could hear Magda quietly going along with my trick.

"I've come to thwart your plans!" I declared.

"My plans to become King?" said Croogy. "Uh, in case you didn't notice, there's a *crown* on my head."

"Your plans to conquer all the other levels by causing Mega Worms to rise up and destroy everything!" I said. "Unless your betrayal of King Zog and the sweet, trusting Slug People is eating you up inside, and you're desperate to confess and surrender yourself for punishment?"

"Don't be ridiculous!" said Croogy. "It's too late for you pathetic humans and for the slimy Slugs! My Moles should be digging through to the creek water any moment, now that we've put a stop to this meddler!"

"Boog!" we heard Boogo say.

"Hi, Boogo."

"How's things, man?" we heard other Moles say.

"Stop talking to him!" yelled Croogy. "He's also an enemy of the—Wait, what's this? Some kind of talking device?"

"You got that right, Croogy!" I yelled triumphantly. "It's been me talking—Doug Underbelly! I'm here at the bottom of the Big Hole with the Slugs! And if you touch the girl, you're going to be in big trouble!"

"Gee, sounds like your boyfriend is really worried about you," said Croogy.

I expected to hear Magda yell "He's not my boyfriend!" But she didn't say anything.

It's possible she was being restrained by Moles.

"Why don't I just reunite the two of you right now? Happy landings, Squirrel." And then we heard Magda scream.

"Dark Eyes!" yelled Ploogoo.

"Magda!" I yelled.

"Boog!" yelled Boogo.

There was a long pause as we all stared up into the blackness of the Big Hole. It was silent. Then we heard something faint. A scream, growing louder. Then we could make out a shape in the darkness, falling toward us.

It was Boogo. His large arms were wrapped around Ploogoo. Whose thinner arms were wrapped around Magda.

Boogo twisted his body so that he took the brunt of the impact. He smashed into the sloping pile of stuff and bounced and tumbled down the side, rolling to rest near the Slugs. Boogo opened his arms to release Ploogoo (who was still screaming), and Ploogoo opened his arms to release Magda. She looked up at the Slugs, aghast.

"All right, I guess you guys were telling the truth about Croogy," said the ambassador. "Y'know, I don't know why we all didn't see it earlier. He seems so obviously bad, doesn't he?"

"Yeah."

"You're right."

"Seems obvious."

Everyone nodded.

"That's what I already—!"

The water streaming down the walls began to intensify.

"The creek! They've almost reached it!" said Ploogoo, getting a hold of his screams.

"Come on, we gotta move this clog," said the ambassador.

The Slug guards reached tiny appendages toward us that were so slippery they were of little value in pulling yourself out of a pit, but we managed to scramble out. Then we all set to work digging at the clog. Magda stared at the guard Slugs working away with their spears.

"Are those giant slugs, Underbelly?" she said. "Why didn't you tell me about the giant slugs?"

"Go say 'Who goes there?' to one of them," I said. "I want to see what happens."

As we dug, Zog asked me more questions about bikes, and I asked him about the Mole throne—was it just my human anatomy, or was the Mole throne excruciatingly painful?

"I never thought about it until you mentioned it," considered Zog, "but yes! It's so painful! Y'know, it was designed by—"

"Let me guess: Croogy," I said, recalling the Royal Advisor's own cushy chair.

Zog snapped his fingers to show I'd hit

the nail on the head. A finger-snap by a giant Mole hand ain't no modest thing like one undertaken by human hands. The sound of it seemed to set the whole area shaking, a shaking which continued to grow in intensity until we realized it was something much bigger than a finger-snap causing the noise.

At that moment a Mega Worm tore into the cavern from below and then disappeared into the ceiling above. He was followed by another, and then lots more. A dozen of them, heading for the surface. The walls of the cavern shook perilously in their wakes.

"We're not moving it fast enough!" yelled Ploogoo, noting the increasing water flow. "We're not going to make it!"

"Perhaps we can help," said a stony voice. I'm not sure if "stony" was an accurate word to describe the voice. I might have picked it subliminally because of who the voice belonged to.

We all looked to see a bunch of Stone Goons standing before us. Also, the Mushroom

King and his tiny son rested on a stone slab that the Goons had dragged along with them. I guess they could live for a while out of the ground, although they didn't seem happy about it.

"You came to help with the clog?" I said.

"If a human is trying to help the Underworlders, it's only right that the Stone Goons should help too," said one Goon.

"We found it very inspirational," said another.

"And we Mushroom Folk knew we couldn't leave it all in your pitiful hands," announced the Mushroom King. "You'd just blow it without us!"

EXPRESSIONLESS

SNOOTY

HARD TO MAKE OUT BUT EVEN MORE SNOOTY

"You tell 'em, Dad!" said the tiny Mushroom. "Haul us close to the pile so we can save you!"

The Stone Goons dragged the slab with the Mushrooms on it next to the clog and then joined in, tearing at the clog with their thick, stony limbs. The Mushroom King and his son pushed their tops against the debris, their jaws set with determination.

"Wow, I never thought I'd see this," said the Slug Ambassador. "You got everyone from all levels working together. Even the Mushrooms! I guess the Great Slugging ain't the only way to pick a decent king."

I was going to say once again that I was no longer the King, but whatever. At that moment I guess I was.

"Hey, weird face!" the tiny Mushroom called to me. "I want more ice cream!"

And then from the Big Hole we all heard the amplified sound of a sudden huge rush of water.

"They've broken through!" yelled Ploogoo.

"Is this thing still working?" Croogy's voice squeaked over the walkie-talkie. I guess he'd figured out which button to press. "Can you hear me over the sound of your watery destiny? Well, I just wanted to say: Happy Worm Day, everybody!"

Everyone dug with everything they had. The Moles with their huge digging hands, the

Slugs with their spears, the Goons with their stony limbs, the Mushrooms with their heads, and us humans with whatever we'd found in the pile. I seemed to have some knack for bringing members of differing groups together to tackle problems I'd created.

We were all working away as one until suddenly . . .

FOOOOOSH!

The clog gave way!

We all leapt to the side as the mountain of stuff collapsed into the hole! Within seconds it had all disappeared into the darkness below.

"Goodbye, beautiful things . . ." said Zog softly.

The sound of rushing water grew deafening, and a moment later a huge rush of water began gushing past us down the hole.

"WE DID IT!" I yelled.

"*You* did it, King!" said Oog. "You save everyone!"

"You're all welcome!" yelled the Mushroom King.

"Yeah. You did good, Underbelly," said Magda. She came forward with outstretched arms.

"Kiss!!" yelled Oog, and the others joined in. "Kiss! Kiss! Kiss!"

"Don't you dare!" I said.

"Get ahold of yourself, Underbelly, I was just giving you a hug! But forget it!"

"No, it's okay," I said. "I mean, we did just sort of save the world. Maybe a little hug is in order."

One of the Stone Goons was closest to me, so he reached over and gave me a hug that felt like falling onto the highway from an overpass.

He handed me back my mac 'n' cheese container.

Then Magda and I hugged, and the bizarre assembly of Moles, Slugs, Goons, and Mushrooms made variations of an "Awwww" sound, as if two long-lost halves of the same whole had at last come together. But they didn't know anything, we were pretty much the only two humans they'd ever met, so they had no context to judge whether we were exactly the same or complete opposites. All they could tell was that we were both humans and both seemed destined to be surrounded by a certain amount of weird.

"*Snort*, 'Happy Worm Day' . . ." said the Slug Ambassador. "What a lousy line."

"Boooooog!" said Boogo.

I broke the hug quickly. I was still panting from the exertion of digging, and the last thing I wanted was Magda getting any dumb ideas that my sweating and pounding heart were because of her.

"King thirsty?" asked Oog. "For first time we have water down here that not have mud in it!"

"You know what?" I said. "There's perfectly good mud water here that looks pretty sweet to me."

Watching the creek water rush past I couldn't help but think there was probably some cool metaphor about releasing all the garbage and letting nature flow or something, but I couldn't think of one. But for the first time I did think that maybe this whole Mole People experience hadn't been so bad, and maybe I did feel some of the sense of belonging that I'd been searching for. I took a swig of the mud water.

"Oh wait," said Oog, "here's a leftover soda from the machine."

I spewed out the mud water.

Then we stopped. We'd all heard a sound. The sound of something enormous. It was coming from below and was so loud we could hear it over the rushing water.

And up through the hole, through the falling waves, exploded what could only have been a very, very adult worm.

FINAL TRANSPORTATION VEHICLE COMPARISON: SIZE OF A STEAM SHIP →

Its giant head swung toward me and I jumped back, smashing my head on a stalactite.

Everyone burst into laughs.

"I was wrong!" I heard the Slug Ambassador cackle. "Your King *is* hilarious!"

And then I passed out to the sound of everyone's deep and heartfelt laughter.

13

BACK TO NORMAL

A few weeks later things were more or less back to "normal" both aboveground and below.

Above, the earth dried up and the Mega Worms returned beneath the surface, just as a bunch of scientists arrived to observe them and then call us liars when there was no proof of their existence. Even the holes they'd caused when they exploded from below had mysteriously vanished.

And below, Oog, Boogo, and Ploogoo had returned King Zooooooooooooooooog to his throne. The Moles were so happy to have him back they forgot all about their plans to take

over anything and went back to being peaceful and liking humans. Everyone agreed they'd all just got caught up in a contagious wave of emotion, as Moles have a habit of doing, and decided a contagious wave of apologies to the Slugs and each other would be the right follow-up.

They even forgave Croogy somewhat, even after all his duplicities had been explained. They busted him back down to "Crog" and initially wanted to strap him to that ridiculously huge Worm and send him to the bottom of the earth, but I convinced them that maybe he had a good center and that all his sourness might just come from the pain of having lost something he loved. I suggested that instead of punishing him they stick him in a room with a couple dozen baby mole pets and see if that softened him up.

Apparently for the first couple of days all Crog did was wail in cliché defeated-bad-guy phrases like "I'll get you for this!" and "Don't you know who I am?" But as the cute mole pets jumped and cuddled and licked his face he eventually gave in and even took one as his pet to replace the one he'd lost so long ago. It turned out that didn't quite satisfy the Moles, though, and a contagious wave of "Let's give him an actual punishment after all" spread through their ranks.

The Royal Guard were reinstated and given back their rightful number of Os. In fact, they all got rewarded for their bravery with an extra O and were now Ooog, Boogoo, and Ploogooo. They wanted to give me an extra O in "Dooug" too, and I said what the heck. It was a little different, and what was wrong with that?

Back at school, all the "hole kids" continued to blather on about having been stuck inside holes. To have been trapped in a hole became a major point for popularity, and the hole kids were so enamored with themselves that they all picked each other for their "Most Interesting Person" assignments.

Magda was doing fine too. King Zoooooooooooooooooog wanted to continue building new relations with the humans and needed a Human Ambassador to collaborate with. I told them I was undergoing intensive therapy for giant Worm trauma and had no interest in the job, so they made Magda the ambassador. Her ping-pong eyes never bounced more vibrantly.

I wrote a note and used my classic fake armpit scratch to launch it at the Human Ambassador's desk. The note read: "So what punishment did they decide on for Crog?"

Magda tossed back this:

CLEANING UP EVERY DROP OF WATER ON THE WORM LEVEL

OLD, UN-ABSORBANT MOP

"HAPPY WORM DAY!"

"Again with you two passing notes," droned Miss Chips without looking up. How did she do it? "Magda, since you're so interested in disrupting the class, why don't you get up and give us your 'Most Interesting Person' report?"

Magda stood and gave me her trademark knowing look. She kept giving it to me as she walked to the front of the class, and then gave it to me some more from there. She opened her notebook, and I started getting a horrible suspicion about what was coming.

"The most interesting person I know is a person who has spent some time trapped in a hole," she began.

The class wasn't impressed by this, since being trapped in a hole was pretty common lately. But I had a sneaking suspicion she wasn't talking about any of them.

"In fact, he spends a lot of time underground," she continued. "Believe it or not, he lives in a graveyard. He wears a big rock on his head. And he has friends who look like they belong in horror movies!"

The kids stopped fidgeting. She had their attention.

Come on, Magda! I thought to myself. I may have become a little more accepting of uniqueness, but I still needed to walk among these guys without a bull's-eye on my head!

"The place he lives in is surrounded by bats and dead trees, and the man he lives with is writing a book about how to cook eels. He's well acquainted with worms and mushrooms, and if you met him in a dark alley you'd probably run screaming!"

Okay, that was a little over-the-top.

My classmates' mouths hung agape. I put my head on my desk and covered it with my arms.

"Trust me, you're never going to meet anybody more interesting than this guy! And his name is . . . Mr. Broom!"

Nobody reacted.

"He's this dead guy that used to own a pickle factory!"

The class erupted in laughter over this revelation. Miss Chips immediately gave Magda an F because the Most Interesting Person was supposed to be someone alive. Magda argued that this stipulation was never made clear, and I defended her by saying that I too had picked a dead person named Mrs. Trout who was interesting because she'd been impaled by a killer moose who was possibly still at large. Then I told Miss Chips that I understood that she was actually a good person inside and was just bitter because of the failure of her fund-raiser with the Brillo pads, and that maybe she just needed a friend. The kids burst into more laughs, and Miss Chips looked at me like she didn't know what I was talking about and then closed her eyes and made snore sounds. I guess she wasn't bitter, she was just being herself.

The class grew emboldened by Miss Chips's snoring and tried to put Magda and me in a weirdness circle right there in the classroom until the bell rang and freed us all, including Miss Chips.

Outside, Simon traded me some Juicy Fruit for a piece of eel gum (my dad's way of combining our interests), and I headed home with Magda in full view of everyone. The water in Cross Creek had returned to normal levels after some hasty underground work, puzzling the local environmentalists, who decided to blame it on melting icebergs or something.

I'd returned to my regular level of unpopularity, so everything was back to "normal." Not really the normal I'd been aiming for, but by this point I was happy to have it. I'd been left with the understanding that being just a bit different wasn't so bad, and you could accept it into your life with little to no increase in ridicule or wedgies.

I didn't even mind seeing the familiar crown symbol as I parted ways with Magda and headed up the Dreadsville Manor walkway. That shape used to give me hives, but now it was just a fun little memory. Ooog stepped out from behind the tree wearing a trench coat.

"TGIF!" he bellowed.

"It's actually Friday! You finally got it right!" I said.

"Check it out!" he said, doing a spin. "Underbelly like Ooog's coat? Ooog wear it to blend in!"

"It's very stylish. Except that garden hose isn't a belt. And that tire isn't a hat."

I asked how everyone was doing in the Mole kingdom and Ooog said great. Mole pets were legal now so they had to come up with a stoop-and-scoop law, Boogoo was teaching little Moles introductory digging, and Ploogooo was going on a date with the girl with the forehead horn.

"Ha! Ploogooo *did* protest too much!" I laughed. "How's King Zooooooooooooooooog doing on the throne? Did he redesign it to be easier on the butt?"

"Oh, right, Ooog almost forget," said Ooog.

"Do you know what 'abdicate' mean?"

I had a sneaking suspicion.

"King disappear again," said Ooog, "but we pretty sure it not Slugs this time. We find this."

He pulled out a bike pump.

"No," I said. "No way."

"We think Zog go to find self on cross-country bike journey. So, great news! Zog hand crown back to you, King Doug! I mean, King Dooug!"

"Nope, uh-uh, forget it," I said.

"And bad news: there emergency!"

"No!"

"Some terrible thing happening . . ."

"No!"

". . . way down on level of Sentient Slime!"

And that's when it finally sank in. Abnormal was always going to be my normal. Weirdness was just never going to stop being part of my life. The only choice left for me was to make sure I accepted it with as much calm and dignity as possible.

PAUL GILLIGAN lives above ground with his wife and kids in Toronto, Canada, where he writes and draws funny things, including the syndicated comic strip *Pooch Café*. He thinks eels are delicious.

paulgilligan.com

RING!
RING!